A HEART FULL OF LOVE

A COLLECTION OF ROMANTIC SHORT STORIES

JK LARKIN

CONTENTS

1

A PERFECT SOLUTION

DEBBIE DE LOUISE

Loser. If you looked up the definition for that term in Mary Jane Hopkin's personal dictionary, her name would be listed and if there were illustrations, her photo might appear there, too. For the twenty-nine years and 358 days that she'd been on this Earth, Mary Jane had accomplished very little. She'd managed to graduate high school only because Mrs. Palmer, her English teacher in her senior year, felt pity for her and gave her a C minus as her final grade. Mary Jane wasn't stupid, but she had such low self-esteem that she failed at everything she tried. An only child, her parents gave her everything she desired except self-confidence.

The list of Mary Jane's failures could fill a book. Since childhood, she'd taken lessons in a variety of wind, string, percussion, and electronic instruments—piano, violin, guitar, drums, flute, electric keyboard, even xylophone. After her parents invested thousands of dollars in lessons, she could barely play a note. Her mother, Gladys, suggested to her father that maybe music wasn't Mary Jane's thing. Then followed years of art lessons at a prestigious art school. A four-year-old could better master her stick drawings and splattered paintings. Her dad then considered that his dear daughter might be more athletic than artistic. She took horseback lessons but couldn't stay on the horse's back. She tried tennis, soccer, softball, basketball, golf, and even ping-pong but constantly lost or broke the balls in each game. She nearly drowned during her Red Cross swimming lesson. Both parents agreed it might be best not to enroll her in skydiving or mountain climbing classes.

After Mary Jane's attempts at enrichment classes failed, her parents tried a different tact. When Mary Jane turned thirteen, her mother told her father that she read some books on teenagers that said they should be allowed to "sink or swim." Her dad pointed out that, judging by MJ's previous swimming lessons, that sink was more likely. Gladys explained that the saying wasn't literal. It simply meant their daughter needed to try things on her own and suffer the consequences if they didn't work out for her. They encouraged Mary Jane to join clubs at school—cheerleading, chess, chorus, and even camera club. She forgot the one-word cheers, had no understanding of the chess rules, got laryngitis her first day at chorus, and dropped and broke the camera club's five-hundred-dollar camera.

It only got worse as Mary Jane grew older. She wasn't asked to her senior prom. Although she wasn't ugly, she was as plain as her middle name portended. For her sixteenth birthday, her mother treated her to a makeover at a local beauty parlor. She was allergic to the cosmetics and broke out in hives. Her dad gave her money for a new wardrobe, but the materials of the new outfits made her itch.

As the years passed, Mary Jane applied to jobs that didn't require a college degree. She was hired as a waitress but spilled soup in a customer's lap. She was a receptionist at a doctor's office but put the wrong patient's chart in the files. She even, without her parents' knowledge, danced at an adult club, but she slipped on the floor and broke her ankle.

Approaching her thirtieth birthday, all Mary Jane wanted was to excel at something. That's why, when she saw the advertisement in her email, hope blossomed in her heart. She knew it had to be authentic because her spam filter hadn't blocked it.

Do you wish you could change your life? For only $99.95, we'll send you the details of our proven plan, A Perfect Solution. Whether you want a high-paying job, a loving spouse, or to win the lottery, if you dream it, you can have it. A Perfect Solution has helped thousands of shy, depressed, self-conscious men and women overcome their feelings of worthlessness.

The final line really grabbed her:

You can even gift A Perfect Solution to a friend or relative or even yourself for your next birthday. A Perfect Solution will arrive in a discreet brown paper package within a week of order with complete instructions and a sixty-day money-back guarantee. Click here to order.

Mary Jane quickly clicked the order link. She had a hundred dollars left in her bank account from her parents' last birthday gift, so she could afford to charge it. She filled out the order form and added her credit card information. She kept her fingers crossed that she'd receive *A Perfect Solution* by her birthday the following week.

During the week, Mary Jane couldn't contain her excitement. Each day, she ran to the door when the mail carrier arrived. It was easy when her parents were at work but, on weekends, she knew she'd have to keep a closer eye out for the mail truck or one of her parents might see her package. Even though the ad claimed that *A Perfect Solution* would be mailed in a discreet box or envelope, she couldn't take any chances. She'd once sent for a magical beauty formula she'd seen described in a woman's magazine at the super-market checkout counter, and her mother never let her live down the mud mask that she received that was closer to the wet dirt in their backyard than it was to a cosmetic product.

The day after she'd ordered *A Perfect Solution*, she didn't expect to receive the package, but Old Carter told her, as he handed her bills and advertisements, that he was going on vacation and that another mail carrier would be taking his route that week. Mary Jane was upset by this news because she feared the mail might be misdelivered, so she made an even greater point of watching for the daily deliveries.

The following day when Carter's vacation started, Mary Jane had just finished lunch when she spotted a blue-uniformed man making his way up her walk. He was younger and taller than Carter with dark hair under his mail hat and light blue eyes that met hers when she opened the door.

"Hi, there Miss," he said handing her a few letters. "I'm taking Carter's route this week. My name is Doug."

Mary Jane smiled and hoped the glint off her adult braces wouldn't blind the new mailman. "Nice to meet you, Doug. I'm Mary Jane. You don't happen to have a package for me, do you?"

Doug shook his head. "I'm afraid not, Mary Jane. That's a very nice name by the way."

"Thank you." She was disappointed but told herself it was only the second day after her order.

The following day, when Doug brought the mail, all he handed her were a few envelopes for her parents. He noticed her expression and said, "Sorry your package isn't here yet, Mary Jane. I'll keep an eye out for it."

"Thank you, Doug. I appreciate that."

The next day, Mary Jane felt like putting on some nice clothes to greet Doug instead of going to the door in her old pajamas and robe. She dug around in her closet and found a dress she'd never worn. She remembered worrying that the material would be scratchy on her skin, but when she put the cream-colored silk on, it glided across her body. She added some stockings and even a dab of lip gloss. *It would be nice to receive A Perfect Solution looking her best*, she thought.

Doug rang the bell. When she answered, he produced a bouquet of carnations and lilies from behind his back. "For you," he smiled, displaying a dimple. "There's no mail for you today, so I thought you might need some cheering up."

"How thoughtful," Mary Jane said taking the flowers tentatively. The previous time she'd received flowers was from her grandmother on her high school graduation. She'd had a sneezing fit but that was twelve years ago. Doug's flowers didn't even water her eyes.

"I must say you look as lovely as those flowers," Doug added. "I hope your package comes soon."

The rest of the week, Mary Jane tried on new clothes before taking in the mail. Each time, Doug had a small gift for her– a box of chocolates on Wednesday, a pretty fan on Thursday, and a lovely gold letter opener on Friday–but *A Perfect Solution* wasn't in his mail sack.

"Tomorrow is my last day before Carter comes back," Doug told her. "I'll say a special prayer tonight that your package arrives."

Mary Jane was touched by this thought. "That's so sweet, Doug. Tomorrow is my birthday."

The mailman smiled, showing his cute dimple again. "Then it has to come. But, if it doesn't, I'll be sure to bring you a special present to celebrate."

"You've brought me so many presents already." Mary Jane was sad she hadn't received *A Perfect Solution*, but she was sadder that tomorrow would be the last day she'd see Doug.

When Mary Jane woke up on her birthday, her parents were

home because it was Saturday. Her mother made her a special breakfast of her favorite chocolate chip pancakes and her father handed her an envelope across the table. It contained another hundred dollars that she could deposit into her bank account to cover the amount she'd spent on *A Perfect Solution*. She hoped she hadn't been a victim of another scam like the mud makeup.

"What's the matter, dear?" Gladys asked. "You're not eating much of your birthday pancakes, and you seem worried about something."

"It's nothing, Mom," she denied. "It's just that I can't believe I'm thirty already."

"You're still very young, MJ," George said. "And, by the way, I've noticed you've been wearing some new clothes lately and you've done something nice to your hair."

"Thanks, Dad. I think it's time for a change."

Just then, the doorbell rang.

Her parents both stood up, but Mary Jane insisted on answering.

Doug was at the door with two packages. Her heart leaped at the sight of him and the two brown envelopes.

"Happy Birthday, Mary Jane," he said, his blue eyes twinkling. "I have two packages for you. Would you mind if you open them in front of me?"

Even though Mary Jane could hardly stand the suspense, she remembered her manners. "Of course, I'll open them in front of you, Doug, but why don't you come in first and meet my parents?"

Gladys and George were happy to meet the young mail carrier. Gladys served him one of the chocolate chip pancakes that was left over, and he complimented her on her cooking. Afterward, George showed Doug his stamp collection, and Doug told him he was also a philatelist.

Mary Jane was happy to see Doug and her parents enjoying

one another's company, but she was eager to open *A Perfect Solution* and the other envelope, which was just labeled with her name.

When Doug finally said he had to finish his route, Mary Jane followed him outside with the envelopes.

"Please open the one with just your name on it first," Doug said. "It's a gift from me."

"I told you that you didn't need to give me any more gifts from you," she said as she slit open the envelope with the gold letter opener he'd given her. Inside was a folded piece of paper. It said, "Will you come to dinner with me tonight?"

Mary Jane felt herself blush. She noticed Doug's cheeks were reddening, too.

"Don't answer yet," Doug said. "Open the second envelope. I know you've been waiting a long time for it."

Mary Jane's fingers were trembling. She was surprised *A Perfect Solution* would come in such a package. She'd expected a large box, but her mother always used to tell her that the best things often came in small packages. She slit open the envelope. Inside was another note, but this one was computer generated. She suspected a hoax. Her stomach dropped as she read the message:

Thank you for purchasing A Perfect Solution. Here are your instructions. As promised, this is a foolproof plan for getting everything you want.

Several spaces below that message was one line of instructions: *Never give up and recognize opportunities when they present themselves.*

She looked up at Doug who was watching her expectedly.

"So, did you get what you wanted?" he asked.

Mary Jane smiled, her adult braces shining like diamonds. "I believe I have and, yes, I'll go to dinner with you tonight, Doug."

Debbie De Louise is an award-winning author and a reference librarian at a public library on Long Island. She is a member of Sisters-in-Crime, International Thriller Writers, the Long Island Authors Group, and the Cat Writers' Association. Her novels include the five books and three stories of the *Cobble Cove* cozy mystery series, a comedy novella, *When Jack Trumps Ace*, a paranormal romance, *Cloudy Rainbow*, and the standalone mysteries; *Reason to Die*, *Sea Scope*, and *Memory Makers*. Her latest book, *Pet Posts: The Cat Chats* is a non-fiction pet book. She lives on Long Island with her husband, daughter, and three cats.

Debbie's stories and poetry also appear in *The Red Penguin Collections*, *What Lies Beyond* and *'Tis the Season*. Her poems are also featured in the Nassau County *Voices In Verse* 2020 anthology and the 2020 *Bards Annual*.

https://debbiedelouise.com

2

CRACKERJACK PROPOSAL

SUZANNE BAGINSKIE

In my senior year, I rode a public service bus to high school every weekday and sat with my friend, Betty, who went to Catholic school. She had a crush on a student from a vocational-technical school, who boarded six blocks after me. By then all seats were taken. Tall with blond wavy hair, he'd hold onto a ceiling strap and lingered above us. Whenever the bus slowed, he swayed in the crowded quarters.

Betty had confided in me that she would like to know him better. When I exited at my stop, I'd always offer him the seat. He never refused. Betty's brown eyes would brighten as he sat, but she couldn't bring herself to utter a word to him. On the return trip home, she made all kinds of excuses to me for not speaking with him. So he never knew.

Most Friday nights, I attended the local Catholic church dances for teens supervised by the nuns with Betty. One evening, we were standing around talking on the edge of the dance floor and I saw Alex enter. Betty blushed and giggled, chattering about how she'd feel if he'd ask her to dance.

He surveyed the crowded room and soon strolled in our direction. She squeezed my arm and smiled.

He approached us both and said, "Hey, I'm Alex. I wanted to thank you for giving me your seat every day." His emerald eyes sparkled, and he studied my face. I'd never noticed them before.

"You're welcome. I'm Suzanne, and this is Betty." She smiled at him. He turned and mumbled, "Hi." Then he stared back at me. A popular slow song started playing in the background.

"Suzanne, would you like to dance?" Shocked, I hesitated and searched Betty's face. She nodded, indicating I should.

"Okay." I followed him onto the dance floor. Betty's smile faded into a frown. She turned and joined a couple of girls seated at a table. My stomach knotted. I didn't want to hurt her, but I couldn't help myself. When Alex grabbed my hand, it sent waves of electric current tingling under my skin. He pulled me close and my cheeks burned.

I'd never really paid much attention to him on the bus. He was Betty's crush, not mine. And then I saw Betty with her arms around another boy, and she smiled at me as they danced past. I relaxed. The song seemed to last forever, and my heart was singing. It was an instant attraction.

He must have felt the same that night because a couple of months later, he asked me to go steady. I proudly wore his black onyx 'A' initial ring. In the meantime, Betty was happy with her new crush and I didn't lose her as a friend. Somehow things turned out well.

Alex and I dated and kept attending those weekly dances, but on Saturday nights he took me to the drive-in theater movies. On our first trip there, I discovered we both loved French fries and Cracker Jack's. He was amused by how eagerly I searched for the elusive prize in each box.

We'd take turns sticking our hands into the caramel-coated

popcorn and peanut mix, but he'd always let me find the prize. Alex chuckled each time I pulled out the tiny, sealed envelope and squealed in delight. I'd tear it open and add the prize to my treasured collection.

After we both graduated, I found employment as a hairdresser and he joined the army. Vietnam and the current war were a hot topic. His father had been a career Navy man. I begged him not to go, but he was stubborn and wanted to serve his country. It broke my heart when Alex left for Ft. Belvoir, but I kissed him good-bye, promised to wait and write daily letters.

After eight weeks of basic training, his parents invited me for the long drive to go visit him. While there, Alex mentioned they scheduled him for paratrooper training in Georgia, and then he'd ship out for Vietnam. I smiled, while tears threatened. A month later before he left the fort, he came home on his first three-day pass.

Alex picked me up, and like old times we went to the drive-in theater. He even thought to bring along a box of Cracker Jack. I was impressed. As we watched the movie and chatted, we both took handfuls from the box. As usual, I searched for the prize. He'd laugh. When the box was half empty, I said, "I don't think this one has a prize." Alex's face became serious. He straightened, grabbed the box from me, and opened the car door. Using the interior light, he started dumping the remaining cracker jacks onto the ground.

"Alex, it's not that important. Close the door, I'm freezing." Frantically, he looked at me and then at the box as he continued to empty it. I shook my head, wondering what was happening.

Pretty soon he closed the door and said, "Check again, the prize is in there." A silly grin spread across his face. He handed me the box. I reached inside and my fingers crawled down the sides to the very bottom and I hit something metal-like and gooey.

"I found it, but it's not wrapped," I said. In the darkness of the car, I lifted out a sticky ring. It didn't feel like a toy. I held it up to catch the outdoor lighting and saw it sparkle. It was a silver band with a centered diamond. "What's this?" I asked. I felt myself blush, and it all made sense why he had dug so desperately inside the box. My heart beat faster.

"Suzanne, I can't get down on my knees in this car. But I want to ask you, will you marry me?" I laughed, said yes, and slipped on the ring. We were engaged and I hugged and kissed him. He served his time in the Army, and six months later we were married.

We've just celebrated our fifty-fifth wedding anniversary, and I've never forgotten his Cracker Jack proposal and self-inserted prize. Cracker Jack has been in business for over one hundred years. Alex and I still share them and our love for each other, and he always allows me to search for the prize.

Suzanne Baginskie recently retired from a law office as an office manager/paralegal after twenty-nine years. She has sold several mysteries and romance stories to anthologies and twenty non-fiction stories to *Chicken Soup for the Soul* books and two *Cup of Comfort* books. Her work appears in Woman's World, Plan B Magazine, The Wrong Side of the Law, two Daily Flash Fiction volumes, First Magazine, True Romance Magazine, and Futures Magazine. She is I'm a member of MWA, FMWA and Sisters-in-Crime and The Short Mystery Fiction Society.

3

ELEVATOR MUSIC

JOHN M. FLOYD

Sally Purvis believed in Fate. She believed that those who are meant for each other will somehow find each other.

But, when Sally stepped into the elevator on the first morning of her new job, her mind wasn't on Fate. It was on her watch, and her appearance, and the butterflies in her stomach. Still, she couldn't help noticing the blond man standing beside her—and the fact that he had a problem.

He had his collar upturned and a suit coat draped over one arm; he was trying to tie a necktie using the mirrored back wall of the elevator.

Before going back to his task, he gave her a sheepish grin—a grin that made Sally say something that, under different circumstances, she would never have dreamed of saying.

"Fashion problem?" she asked.

The grin faltered. "Fashion crisis. Sales meeting in ten minutes and I spilled coffee on my tie in the car." He loosened a lopsided knot and started over again.

"I don't see a stain," she said.

"This one's a spare from my glove compartment, but it's too old and too wide."

She pushed the button for eighteen. The doors sighed shut.

"Here, let me try," she said. "I have three brothers."

Fifteen seconds later she finished off a passable half-windsor, gave it a final tug, and smoothed his collar. "There. You have a perfect dimple."

"You have two of them."

For a moment their eyes locked.

"I meant in your tie," she said. They both smiled.

The elevator car slowed, then stopped. They faced forward. Sixth floor.

The doors opened; nobody there. Seconds later they closed again.

The blond man pulled his jacket on. "Thanks for the help."

"You're welcome." Sally was watching the digital floor numbers above the door.

"You work here in the building?" he asked.

"It's my first day. I'm a little nervous." She turned to look at him. "What about you?"

"Am I nervous?"

She grinned again. "Do you work here?"

"Twelve years," he said.

"What do you do?"

"I'm a salesman."

"What do you sell?"

"Anything the company makes," he said.

The elevator stopped again, on nine. A middle-aged woman got on and nodded to him. He nodded back. She got off on ten.

Sally said, "One of your customers?"

"Everybody's a customer."

She stared at the closing doors. "You like speaking in generalities, don't you."

"Oh, I don't know. I can be specific."

"Let's hear it," she said.

"Antonio's. Corner of Hamilton and Fourth."

"Excuse me?"

"Go to lunch with me," he said.

She turned and looked him in the eye. He seemed to be holding his breath.

"Okay," she said.

He exhaled, and smiled again.

"Should I meet you there?" she asked.

"I'll stop by your office. Where'll you be working?"

"Eighteen. Accounting."

He blinked. "You're with Cameron Enterprises?"

"How'd you know?"

"We have the top three floors."

"You work there too?"

"Don't look so shocked."

"I'm not," she said. "I just . . ."

He waited.

"I wondered if they might frown on . . . well—"

"Fraternization in the ranks?" he asked.

She blushed a little.

"You tied my tie," he said, "and I asked you to lunch. We're not engaged or anything."

"Darn," she said.

Again Sally looked up at him, and he looked back. She felt her face grow warm. If this were a movie, she thought, violins would be playing.

Then she drew a deep breath and concentrated on the floor

numbers. She assumed he was going to nineteen; it was the only other button lit up.

"What time?" he asked. "For lunch."

"I'm not sure. I have a meeting at eleven on the twentieth floor."

"With the brass?"

"I guess. Introductions, they said."

He nodded. "Standard procedure, the first day."

"The twentieth floor," she repeated. "Sounds intimidating."

"It is, in a way."

"Are you there a lot? As a salesman?"

"As little as possible."

She frowned, thinking. "They're not a bad bunch, are they?"

"They're pretty good, actually. Everybody here is."

"Generalities again. Sure you're not a lawyer?"

"Positive." He studied her face. "11:45," he said.

"What?"

"I'm being specific again. That's when I'll pick you up."

The elevator stopped. Eighteenth floor.

"What if they're not done with me by then?" she asked.

"Tell them they have to be."

They stood there a second, smiling at each other. He looked nervous too, she thought.

She swallowed. "I'm Sally."

"Tom."

The doors opened. "Accounting," she said, backing out into the hallway.

"I'll remember."

The doors closed between them.

∼

During the next three hours, Sally learned that Cameron Enterprises had sixty-two employees, twenty of them in marketing, on the nineteenth floor. None of the salesmen was named Tom.

Sally stewed over it the rest of the morning. She finally decided, on the elevator to the twentieth floor at 10:55, that it would all soon be clear. She thought Fate had a hand in this, with or without violin music.

An attractive older woman met her outside the CEO's office on twenty. "I'm Mary," she said. "Mr. Cameron's assistant."

Sally followed her into a huge corner office. Beyond the windows was a panoramic view of the city. The head of the company rose from his desk as they entered.

"Ms. Sally Purvis," the assistant said, "Mr. Thomas Cameron."

Sally's jaw dropped as Mary left the room.

"Tom?" she murmured.

"I got three compliments on the tie," he said. "How are you at fixing budget problems?"

Sally broke out a smile. "I thought marketing was on nineteen."

"It is. I met with them there, this morning."

"You said you were a salesman."

He grinned. "Everyone here's a salesman." He walked around the desk and took her hands in his. "Generally speaking."

She swallowed, looking into his eyes. "Do you believe in Fate, Tom Cameron?"

"I believe in early lunches," he said.

She realized, as they left together, that her nervousness was gone.

John M. Floyd's work has appeared in more than 300 different publications, including *Alfred Hitchcock's Mystery Magazine*, *Ellery Queen's Mystery Magazine*, *Strand Magazine*, *The Saturday Evening Post*, and three editions of *The Best American Mystery Stories*. John is also an Edgar Award finalist, a four-time Derringer Award winner, the 2018 recipient of the Edward D. Hoch Memorial Golden Derringer Award, and the author of nine books.

www.johnmfloyd.com

4

WEAPONS AREN'T MADE

SKYE BALLANTYNE

The soldiers were getting closer, soon they would be on top of the couple. There was nowhere else left to turn. Allen stared at Felicia, his eyes filled with the knowledge of what was about to happen, what had to happen. Felicia couldn't bear to look at him. It was too painful. She clenched her teeth to press out the pain she was feeling. She couldn't afford to have her emotions get in the way.

"Hey," Allen said, putting one hand on Felicia's waist, while using his other hand to gently turn Felicia's face towards his. "It's going to be okay." He held her head steady with his hand.

Felicia stared at Allen, their eyes both filled with the knowledge of what she had to do. They had planned this. It was better this way. At least those were the words Felicia kept reminding herself of.

"It's okay," Allen said softly, "It's okay to be scared." He put his head against her forehead. "Being scared just means that you're about to do something really, really brave." Allen took out the dagger. "I was never meant to be your hero." He wrapped Felicia's fingers around the dagger. "You were always meant to be mine." Letting Felicia hold the dagger on her own, Allen placed a kiss on her forehead.

Felicia's eyes fell to the gleaming metal in her hand. She nodded her head and took a deep breath. She would do what she had to do–she couldn't let her village down. She couldn't let the other villages down. She couldn't let her friends or Allen down. No matter how much it hurt, she had a job to do. After all, she was a hero, and heroes don't get the rewards. Heroes pay the price.

With the dagger in hand, Felicia ached to be normal, to have been born a simple village girl, the daughter of an everyday farmer, a girl who could live a simple life. But that wasn't her lot in life. No, she wasn't normal. Her life was always full of bloody knuckles and shards of glass, full of ruling and spying, fighting, she never had the chance to be soft, to be an ordinary person, to be the farmer she so envied. If she did this, all those dreams would die. Any hope, any chance of that kind of life... would die.

Taking a deep breath, Felicia closed her eyes. Tears gathered at the ends of her eyelashes, but she refused to let them fall. As the last bit of air left her lungs, Felicia plunged the dagger into Allen. Allen let out a grunt of pain as he began to fall toward the ground. Felicia wrapped her arms around Allen and gently guided him to the ground.

"No, no, no, no," Felicia cried as she laid his head on the ground. "I'm so sorry." Silently, unable to hold them back any longer, tears slipped from Felicia's eyes.

Allen placed his hand on the hilt of the dagger protruding from his abdomen as blood sputtered from his mouth.

"I'm so sorry," Felicia whispered, her stomach churning with the pain Allen was in.

"Hey," Allen breathed as another spurt of blood spewed from

his mouth, "Don't cry," Allen reached up to wipe away the hair and tears that were masking Felicia's face, caressing her cheek as he did so.

"You did what you had to do," Allen continued, his hand falling back to the ground as his strength waned.

Felicia nodded, putting her hand on top of the dagger as if to hold it in place. With her free hand, she swiped away the rest of the tears. She didn't want Allen's last memories of her to be of her crying. She wanted him to die seeing her smile. She would have the rest of her life to grieve–she wasn't going to do it now. Not in front of him.

"I love you," Felicia said with a sad smile, holding his hand.

"I love you too," Allen's voice was getting softer, "Take care, my little farmer."

As he spoke, what was left of his life slipped away, and his body went limp. His eyes stared blankly into a void.

"No! Allen!" Felicia cried.

She kissed Allen's lifeless lips one more time and got to her feet as the soldiers came into the clearing. Felicia sucked back her tears and stared at the soldiers stonily. She wasn't going to let them see her cry. Her tears were not for them. She squared her shoulders and stared at them with the dignity of a queen. She wouldn't go down with a fight. After all, she was a weapon, and weapons weren't made to weep. They were made to fight.

~

Skye has stories in her heart that just won't be silenced. They need to be shared with others. She has an entire series with the characters from this anthology and the books have just grown with her as she has aged. She hopes that you find as much joy in reading about these characters as she had while she was writing about them.

5

THE THIRD COINCIDENCE

CHRISTINA HOAG

Mattie turned the corner into her street, huffing as she entered the final stretch of her three-mile morning power-walk. She immediately noticed a man lolling against one of the stone pillars bracketing the Moskovitzs' gate across from her house, arms folded, ankles crossed. By the angle of his head, he seemed to be studying her second-story window–her office.

As if sensing she was staring at him, he turned and caught her gaze. She felt a jolt. It was the guy from the fish and chips takeout place last night. He'd pivoted from the counter, bundle wrapped in butcher's paper in hand, and smiled at her as she shuffled forward in the line. Was it the same man? She slowed her pace as her heartbeat quickened.

Mattie considered herself a student of detail. She didn't miss much, or at least she didn't like to think she did. The guy at the fish and chips place had a black leather jacket. This guy was wearing a black leather jacket. Of course, many men wear black leather jackets. The fish and chips guy had a pasty complexion framed by collar-length chestnut brown hair. Like this man. But it was a description that could fit a million youngish men in Queens, let alone the whole of New York City. She was overreacting.

Mattie arrived at the turnoff to her front path. Should she walk on so as not to reveal where she lived? It seemed a bit paranoid. He was now scrolling through his phone. She took advantage of the moment to wheel into the house and throw the deadbolt on the front door. Kew Gardens was a safe neighborhood, but it was still New York.

She climbed the stairs to her office. It was an odd coincidence, but likely a random brushing of elbows. Even in a city of eight million, it happened occasionally. She was reminded of Hercule Poirot's theory of happenstance: "One coincidence is just a coincidence, two coincidences are a clue, three coincidences are proof."

She sat at her desk and started sifting through her inbox. Monday morning brought a barrage of emails, most from weekend internet surfers who'd run across an invitation on Agatha Christie's official website to "ask anything Agatha of our resident Christie expert Prunella Fernsby." Mattie had adopted the very English pseudonym thinking it was more à propos for the job than her very Greek name of Amaltheia Zafeirakis.

She clicked on the first email. "How many times did Agatha Christie use arsenic in her plots?" A common query. Mattie opened her "Poisons" file and copied and pasted her stock answer. "Agatha Christie used poison as her murder method in fourteen novels, more than any other mystery writer. She gained her knowledge from working as a nurse and pharmacy dispenser during both world wars, using a wide variety of lethal substances to off characters, cyanide being her favourite. Arsenic was used in one novel, *4:50 from Paddington*."

Next. "Is Chris Christie related to Agatha Christie?" The former New Jersey governor must've appeared on a Sunday morning news show. At least one of those inquiries came in after he guested on a program somewhere. She again copied and pasted her answer. "Christie was the surname of Agatha's first husband Archibald. There is no known relation between Archibald Christie and Chris Christie."

Then a Hollywood producer wanted to know: "Are film/TV rights available for any Agatha Christie properties?" He'd sent it using a gmail address. If he couldn't afford a company domain and sent a rights query to the trivia inbox, he was unlikely to be a serious producer. "Not at this time. Thank you for your interest," she replied in accordance with the licensing department's instructions.

The toot of a car horn in the street pricked her ears. She pushed herself off the desk to propel her wheeled chair to the window. Black Jacket was getting into a Mini Cooper that had the Union Jack on the back of its side-view mirrors. The Mini zoomed off. Mattie walked her chair back to her desk lost in thought. A British car with the British flag. Stands to reason he was British, which provided a logical explanation for why he was buying fish and chips.

An email sliding into her inbox truncated her train of thought. It was from her boss Penelope, who managed her famous great-aunt's lucrative literary estate. Penelope checked in at this time every Monday morning, late afternoon in the U.K., with her assignments for the week.

"Two scripts have arrived for the first two episodes of the latest ITV Marple adaptation. Please look over by end of week. Several instances of copyright infringement were detected over the weekend from the usual suspects in Eastern Europe. Please review ASAP and we'll send them to Dunbarton if needed. By the way, I'll be popping across the pond for studio meetings in LA soon. I'll stop off in New York so we can finally meet and discuss marketing the first official Agatha Christie tour to Americans. Brilliant idea! Cheers, Plpe."

Mattie felt a boost in spirits. She'd suggested the tour, with herself as chief guide, of course, last month and never received a response. Now it merited an in-person meeting with "Plpe," whom she'd never actually met. She'd interviewed for the job via Skype after Penelope read a story about author superfans, which quoted Mattie, in the New York Times' book section five years ago. A month later Penelope had contacted her asking if she wanted a job handling the flood of trivia questions the Christie estate received.

She'd jumped at the chance, creating the character of Prunella Fernsby, who certainly had never stepped foot in Queens, where Mattie had lived her whole life, except for the first two years in Thessaly, Greece. Mattie made sure her Prunella guise was complete by setting her computer to British English to catch spelling differences. It occurred to her that if Prunella Fernsby were to be the tour guide, she'd have to adopt an English accent. It was doable.

Mattie opened the link to the first copyright infringement. It was from Romania. She clicked on Google translate. She'd done so well at answering trivia that Penelope had expanded her duties to include reviewing scripts to ensure they rang true to Agatha's beloved characters. No sex, nudity, or the like. After Mattie proved her mettle at that task, Penelope assigned her copyright research.

But after compiling a comprehensive library of Agatha facts and reading reams of others' work, Mattie was bored. What she really wanted to do was write a new Miss Marple novel. In fact, she'd already started outlining it. She wondered if she should bring this up during the meeting with "Plpe" as the tour idea had gone over so well. Mattie plucked a Golden Delicious from the bowl of different types of apples on her desk. Its sweetness seemed a just reward for the tour news, and after taking a satisfyingly juicy bite, she settled in to review the latest IP theft.

At 5:30 p.m., Mattie turned off her computer and headed through pelting rain to the George & Dragon, an English pub that featured dark wood paneling, a red phone box, and a dartboard. She hung her raincoat and umbrella on a row of hooks inside the door and greeted the owner, who was standing on a stepstool and draping bunting over the wall lamps.

"' Ow's it goin, ducks? The usual, is i'?" Alf had lived for thirty years in New York, but his speech was still larded with the East End's dropped h's and glottal stops.

"How'd you ever guess?" she said.

It was early still. Only one other customer (punter, as Alf would say) was –a man hunched over the bar, where he was watching the news on the TV on the wall above the liquor shelves.

Alf climbed down from the step stool and, a minute later, brought a sudsy pint of lager to her table where she'd opened her notebook to her plot outline. Alf continued hanging the string of triangular flags.

"What's that for, Alf?" Mattie flicked off the foam mustache the beer left with her tongue.

"Friday's the twenty-third of April, St. George's Day, so we're 'avin' a bit of a knees-up. You'll come, won't yer, love?"

The flags were white with a red cross, the cross of St. George, England's patron saint who slayed a dragon, as legend had it.

"Wouldn't miss it," she said.

"Good girl. 'ow's the wri'in?"

She was about to answer when the door's hinges squealed, and a customer entered. The new punter beelined to the guy at the bar and slapped him on the shoulder, causing him to swivel forty-five degrees on the stool. Mattie stared. Holy shit! It was *him*, the guy from her street this morning. The fish and chips guy.

Alf was already lifting the bridge to get behind the bar. "Wot can I get yer, old son?"

His chitchat dropped away as Mattie focused on the man, who had a pen in his hand. Again, as if sensing Mattie's gaze, he appeared startled at seeing her. She dropped her head and pretended to be absorbed in her notebook as the heat of embarrassment flushed through her chest.

Raising her head just enough to eye the bar, Mattie observed the two men. The new customer drained his beer in a couple of long gulps and then stood, grabbing a fistful of salted peanuts from a bowl on the bar. The other stood as well. They walked to the door, the guy grabbing a black leather jacket from the wall hooks. It *was* him, but she hadn't noticed the jacket because it'd been hanging on the wall opposite her raincoat.

If the fish and chips place was the baseline, seeing him in the street was the first coincidence. This, then, was the second, and, according to Poirot, a clue. She shoved her notebook in her purse. She was going to follow where the clue led her.

The rain had given way to dense fog while she'd been inside the pub. Turning up the large collar of her raincoat, she looked up and down the sidewalk, but could see no one in the filmy air, so she turned into the small parking lot on the right. Two headlights burst through the mist like flares. They were coming straight at her. She jumped out of the way as red and blue stripes flashed by. It was the Mini from this morning. It took Mattie half a second to recover. Then she ran to the sidewalk, but the fog had already swallowed the car. She returned to the pub and leaned over the bar where Alf was drying the used glasses.

"That guy who was just in here, have you ever seen him before?"

Alf slapped the dishtowel over his shoulder. "The Irishman? Can't say I 'ave, ducks."

Mattie frowned. "Irish?"

"Told me 'e's from Derry. Another pint for yer?"

"Not right now, thanks."

Mattie wandered back to her table. After she sat, she noticed something on the floor under the stool the guy had occupied. She crossed the room and picked it up. Just a brewery's cardboard coaster that Alf always used with drinks. As she went to put it back on the bar, she caught sight of its backside. There were two small drawings on it in blue pen. One was a constellation of eight arrows arranged so their points made a square shape. The other was a cross with two horizontal bars with the centerline ending in a sideways eight.

They seemed too specific for random doodles. She sat at her table and took out her phone, typing a description of the arrow drawing into the search field. Results popped right up. A symbol meaning chaos. She tried the other. It was a Leviathan cross, also known as the Church of Satan's cross. Her arms pricked with gooseflesh. Was Black Jacket a devil-worshipper? He looked overwhelmingly normal, but perhaps that was on purpose. She felt the sudden urge for the safety and comfort of home.

"Gotta go, Alf."

"Righto then, love."

Holding her keys between her fingers as a weapon, she raced home, her eyes scanning the street for a Mini Cooper. She locked her front door with all three locks and ran upstairs. She grabbed a Granny Smith from the bowl and bit into it, sucking the mouth-puckering tartness onto her tongue. Gradually, she felt the hummingbird wings of her nerves settling. After taking another bite, she put the apple aside as she remembered what Alf had told her and googled Derry. The second-largest city in Northern Ireland, called Derry by Catholics and Londonderry by Protestants. If he'd said "Derry," he must be a Catholic, which seemed at odds with patronizing an English pub or driving a car with the Union Jack emblazoned on it.

Unless … he was visiting English sites and mulling chaos for a reason. Could he be a member of some Irish republican group? Realization crashed into Mattie's brain. St. George's Day. It would be the perfect day to wreak havoc on English symbols. No one would ever suspect targets in Queens, of all places. She gasped as she felt a second clang. *Queens!* It *was* of all places. And of course, Kew Gardens, named for the royal botanic garden in London and boasting faux Tudor buildings on its main street.

Mattie could scarcely breathe. It made perfect sense. And it was logical that she, an avid anglophile, had stumbled upon it because she frequented English places. That's why Black Jacket reeled at seeing her. Did he suspect she was onto him? Could she be in danger? She took a huge bite of the Granny Smith and crunched her way to calm.

She should call the police. She picked up her phone then paused. She'd had a dim view of the New York Police Department since she'd double-parked outside a bookstore once so she could run in to pick up a pre-ordered Christie biography. She was back in her car and about to leave when a cop knocked on her window saying, "Move the fucking car, lady," like a line out of a bad movie. She could just imagine some cop telling her now, "You're fucking crazy, lady."

Forget the police. Who handled domestic terrorism? The FBI. She found a 24-hour number for the New York office online and called.

"FBI. Special Agent Colmenares. How may I help you?"

Mattie froze. Could this really be a plot or was she seeing connections that weren't there like some conspiracy nut?

"Hello?" the agent said.

Poirot, she reminded herself, and plunged in, striking a suitably dubious tone so as not to come across like a fringe lunatic. "Yes, hi. I think I might've come across some type of IRA plan in Queens."

Agent Colmenares listened to her story. "Do you have a name or location of this suspect?" he asked when she'd finished.

"Well, no."

"Ma'am, I'm not saying there's nothing to this, but we need solid information in order to investigate."

"I have the coaster. It probably has his fingerprints," she offered.

"I'm just the after-hours duty agent but all calls are recorded and reviewed, and if further investigation is warranted, the material is forwarded to the appropriate agent. Do you want to leave your contact information?"

It seemed the proper thing to do. After giving her name, address, and phone number, Mattie hung up and peered through the curtains at the street. Stanley Moskowitz was ambling along the sidewalk with his French bulldog Brigitte, named for Brigitte Bardot. She hurried downstairs to the street.

"Mr. Moskowitz! Sorry to bother you, but there was a man hanging around in front of your house this morning. He seemed a little suspicious."

"Nah, that was probably the fellow who came to look at the apartment in the back."

"Oh." She'd forgotten that Stanley had a small studio setup he rented out. "Is he taking it, the apartment?"

"He said he'd get back to me in a few days. Seemed a nice enough young man. Quiet, the type who'd keep to himself. Believe me, I wouldn't rent to a bad character. I haven't been on this earth for almost nine decades for nothing."

Alarm streaked through her. *Quiet, kept to himself.* That's what neighbors always said about serial killers! Her heart hammered. "Did he leave a name or phone number?"

Stanley scratched his whiskered chin. "I don't recall. At my age, it's a wonder I remember how to get dressed every day. I really don't think he's anything to worry about."

If only he knew! After saying goodbye, she returned inside and ate the rest of the Granny Smith.

Over the following days, Mattie kept a sharp eye out for Black Jacket and the Mini. She returned to the fish and chips shop and the pub, and even sought out other English-related places, such as a tearoom with an adjoining store that stocked British groceries. She didn't see him, nor did she hear from the FBI. She concluded it was all a product of her overactive imagination stimulated by her immersion in the Christie canon.

She was certainly glad she hadn't told anyone, especially her family who thought her passion for Agatha Christie was a form of OCD. They'd been urging her to take a "real job" in the family's growing diner chain since she was a teenager and blamed her obsession as the reason she was still single at forty. They were probably right. Once potential suitors discovered she was into murder mysteries, they seemed to think she was a budding black widow. She'd often thought that if she'd never discovered Agatha Christie books that snowy Saturday afternoon in the library, she'd be happily ensconced in the suburbs with a husband, two kids, and a dog. Instead, she had Miss Marple and Poirot as perpetual companions.

Thursday started as any other day. A walk followed by an apple, a Braeburn, whose sweet-tempered tartness reflected her mood. Her doorbell chimed as she was combing through the trivia query inbox. Looking out the window, she saw a White man and a Black woman dressed in suits. They didn't look like Jehovah's witnesses. Curious, she went down and opened the door.

"Ms. Zafeirakis? I'm Special Agent Veronica Deveraux from the FBI and this is Special Agent David Kovach. We're responding to your call about possible UK targets in New York City."

Mattie was taken aback. "Yes," was all she managed to say.

"We're going to put the George & Dragon under surveillance tomorrow evening. We would like you to be there and signal us if the suspect you observed earlier in the week is present. We haven't been able to locate him."

"Oh. Of course. I was going to go anyway. What... I mean, have you found... evidence or something?"

"We can't divulge that since it's an ongoing investigation. When you see the suspect, don't engage. Move close, then drop your purse next to him, then pick it up like it's an accident. We also have your general description from the phone call."

She closed the door, feeling vindicated. She'd been right! This called for a super-celebratory apple. She bounded up the stairs and ordered a box of purple-colored Black Diamond apples from Tibet online. In the meantime, she'd make do with a Gala from New Zealand, her favorite variety.

The rest of Thursday and Friday passed with agonizing slowness. Late Friday afternoon, she was looking forward to getting to the George & Dragon early when Penelope sent a particularly egregious copyright infringement by a film school student in Australia. She wanted it researched immediately so the lawyers could email the cease-and-desist on Sunday, which would be Monday morning Sydney time. Sighing, Mattie opened the file.

By the time, she got to the pub, it was packed, thanks to Alf's two-for-one special proclaimed on a sandwich board on the sidewalk. She spotted Agent Deveraux sitting in a corner and walked past her. Deveraux subtly nodded toward the far end of the bar. Mattie followed the signal with her eyes and saw Kovach perched on a stool. He rubbed his upper lip in acknowledgment. Mattie felt galvanized. She was in a real-life espionage thriller! She jostled her way through the jam at the bar and waved to Alf.

He barrelled down the bar. "'Ere she is—the famous Prunella Fernsby," he bellowed. His cheeks were flushed and his voice louder than usual. He'd obviously been doing a little celebrating himself. He leaned over the bar and said in a low voice, "The twofer ends in five minutes, but I'll give it to you all night seeing as you're a regular. Just keep it shtum." He tapped the side of his nose and gave her a knowing nod.

She smiled. "Right."

Alf pulled the pint and slipped the beer in front of her with a sloppy hand as he trundled off, hitching his pants, to attend an impatient customer. "Keep yer britches on!"

Mattie dabbed the dribbles of foam from the glass with a napkin and took a sip, wondering how she was going to circulate in this crowd.

"Pardon me, but did I hear correctly that you're Prunella Fernsby?" The voice was male with the crisp enunciation of Etonian English.

Mattie looked at the speaker and spluttered her mouthful of beer.

"So sorry, didn't mean to frighten you," Black Jacket said.

"I'm fine." She wiped her chin with the already soaked napkin. She looked up to find him smiling into her eyes. Mattie felt a pleasant frisson ripple through her.

"I've written to you." He bobbed his head to talk around a large man shoving his way between them. "Twice actually."

Mattie craned her neck to talk around the interloper sandwiched in the middle of them. "You have?"

"I'm Colin McTavidge."

The name seemed familiar, but she couldn't pigeonhole it. "You don't sound Irish." The interloper hiked his eyebrows at her as if to say, "not on your bloody life." "Not you," she said. She peered around him and repeated her statement.

Colin laughed. "That's my friend Liam. I do trivia for the official Sherlock Holmes website, like you do for Agatha Christie," he said.

Shit. Alf must've thought she was asking about the second man in the bar Monday. "Ohmygod, you're *that* Colin McTavidge. I've always wanted to meet you."

A loud groan went up from the crowd. The two-fer special had ended. Colin pointed over the pool of heads, indicating they should move to a quieter area. She gave him a thumbs-up and followed him as he cut a crooked path through the throng to the far side of the room, where there were fewer people.

"Ah, that's better." Colin drilled her eyes with his. "I've always wanted to meet *you*. We're peas of the same pod, you might say, but I imagined you lived in a thatched cottage in the Cotswolds and spent your evenings knitting babies' bonnets with a cat curled on your lap."

It was Mattie's turn to laugh. "I guess my alter ego works then. My real name's Almatheia Zafeirakis, everyone calls me Mattie. I've lived in Queens basically my whole life." She felt a click in her brain. "I remember now. You asked me about similarities between Agatha and Conan Doyle, or if Agatha had been influenced by Conan Doyle, something like that."

"Both actually. I thought I'd save myself some research and go straight to the expert."

"You live here?"

"Manhattan."

"You're forgiven. Don't tell me you live on Baker Street."

"No, but—don't roll your eyes—I did convince the landlord to let me change my apartment number to 221B."

Mattie smiled. "I named my house 'Styles,' for ..."

He held up a finger. "Agatha's first published book, *The Mysterious Affair at Styles*."

She stared at him, feeling sparkles course through her body. She'd never met anyone like herself. "What brings you to the lesser world of Queens?"

"I'm sussing out places for a Sherlock Holmes scavenger hunt. We give people clues to Britishy sorts of places, then people have to figure out where to go, find the clues at the places, and then solve the puzzle at the end. The winner gets a complete set of Conan Doyle. I think we're going to base the next one around Kew Gardens and Queens."

"That explains why I saw you at the fish and chips place and here. But why were you at Stanley Moskowitz's? I live across the street from him."

"Hang on. You saw me at the chippie and the pub and Stanley's, *and* you remember me? You're quite the sleuth. I thought a woman was staring at me here the other day. Anyway, I'm looking for cheap digs to rent here while I set everything up to avoid the long subway journey. I saw Stanley's advert."

"Sorry for staring. What about the coaster with the drawings? I found it on the floor here after you almost ran me over in the Mini."

"That was you in the fog too? Oh god. Sorry. I was glad I didn't run you over then, but now I'm *really* glad. The symbols are possible clues for the hunt. People love symbology." He cocked his head. "Why don't we do the hunt together? People would love a Poirot-Sherlock teamup, or maybe teams—Poirot fans versus Sherlock fans."

"That would be brilliant." Mattie's eyes shone.

"An American who says 'brilliant'! *That's* brilliant. I'm famished, by the way. Have you eaten dinner?"

"Fish and chips, perhaps?"

She sensed movement around them and suddenly realized Deveraux stood on one side of them and Kovach on the other. Shit. She'd forgotten all about them.

Deveraux held up her ID. "Mr. McTavidge? FBI. We need to ask you some questions about Liam Dougherty," she said, pursing her lips in disapproval at Mattie.

"Wait, no. I got it all wrong," Mattie said.

Colin gave her a puzzled look.

"I'm so sorry I thought you were planting a bomb and I called the FBI I'm totally embarrassed I'm really sorry." Her words tumbled together like falling rocks.

"Mr. McTavidge?" Deveraux said.

"Yes, of course." He accompanied the agents outside.

As the door shut behind them, Mattie felt an overwhelming wash of desolation. Colin must think her a total fool. She'd finally found a kindred spirit, a soul twin, and she'd ruined it. She'd completely misread the situation. Why the hell had she called the FBI? Poirot and his little grey cells had betrayed her. She collected her coat and trudged home, feeling an urgent hankering for a Red Delicious.

Mattie spent Saturday eating apples in front of the television. She started to watch a modern adaptation of *And Then There Were None,* but the plot seemed trite and transparent. She switched to another channel. An old black-and-white of *The Hounds of the Baskervilles* was airing, but that only reminded her of her massive faux pas. She couldn't help but feel that her parents, sisters, and cousins had been right all along. Something was wrong with her. She needed help.

Despite waking up with a griping stomach on Sunday, she got herself to the farmers' market to restock her apple supply. Her email pinged just as she was leaving. It was Penelope. "Fantastic news! I've found the perfect Prunella Fernsby to lead the tour! She's the embodiment of Miss Marple! More later, Plpe."

If Mattie's spirits had sunk to sea level, they were now below sea level. She should've known she'd never be allowed to lead the tour. She did an about-face and bought three pounds of Granny Smiths, which she started eating on the way home and spent the rest of the day nursing her stomach. She resolved to call her father that week and ask what she could do at the diner.

The following morning, she couldn't motivate herself to go for her walk. She sat at her desk in her pilled flannel pajamas. She was just about to check the trivia inbox when she heard a thud on the front porch. She went downstairs and opened the door. It was the Tibetan apples she'd splurged on. Total waste of money.

As she bent to pick up the box, she heard her name. She was surprised to see Colin bearing down her garden path with an air of determination. He was coming to chew her out. Well, she deserved it. She braced herself.

"I was hoping to catch you on your walk," he said.

"I'm not feeling so great."

"This will make you feel better. Have you seen the news?"

She shook her head, wondering what the news had to do with anything. He held up his phone screen. She peered at the head-line. "Bomb Plot Disguised as Sherlock Holmes Hunt Busted."

She looked at him, baffled.

"The FBI arrested Liam an hour ago. He's an Irish republican operative and was planning a trail of bombs on the scavenger hunt sites. You're bloody brilliant, Mattie!"

Stunned, all she could do was blink.

"I spent the weekend convincing the FBI that I had nothing to do with any of it. They finally believed me and then they told me not to say anything until they arrested Liam. They already had him on their terrorist list and had heard rumors of a possible operation in New York but didn't connect the two until they looked into your call."

"Poirot's theory worked," Mattie said, feeling the pieces fall into place. "One coincidence is a coincidence, two are a clue, three are proof."

"By the way, are those Black Diamonds you're holding?"

Mattie's eyes widened. "You know about Tibetan purple apples?"

"I adore apples." He took the box from her and they stepped inside. "You know what Sherlock Holmes said about coincidence? 'The universe is rarely so lazy'."

Christina Hoag is the author of novels *Girl on the Brink*, named to Suspense Magazine's Best YA list, and *Skin of Tattoos*, Silver Falchion Award finalist. A former journalist, she reported from Latin America for Time, Business Week, Financial Times, New York Times, Sunday Times of London, Miami Herald, Houston Chronicle and others. In 2020, she won prizes for essay and short story in the International Human Rights Arts Festival Literary Awards and for essay and novel excerpt in the Soul-Making Keats Writing Competition. Her short fiction and creative nonfiction have been published in literary journals including Shooter (UK), San Antonio Review, Round Table Literary Journal and Lunch Ticket. For more information and book purchases, visit www.christinahoag.com.

6

THE POWER OF A SMILE

JIM TRITTEN

She stood there, the cutest whimsical smile on her face. She had wrapped me around her little finger. Knowing I was hooked became part of the rush of loving feelings I experienced that morning. She leaned her head to the right. Her smile broadened, and I knew she knew she would get a reaction. I broke out in a wide grin and marveled at the sight. She stood there, leaning against the railing, in a pink and white outfit with an outlandish white hat. She was going to be in my life forever. I walked over and hugged her.

As she took off her hat with a flourish and continued to smile, I realized I was being manipulated. I loved it. I was along for the ride. There had been, and there would be, other females that would pass through my life, but this one... this one certainly was different. It would be a never-ending relationship–we were destined to be intertwined for life. Our connection was at a peak right now–I was a huge part of her world–but it was fated to ebb and flow through time. Today, this morning, all she could see was my presence, and I knew it to be welcome and comforting. Would she always think so? Would my being there please her in years to come?

That morning was a time for complete mindfulness, a moment not to be concerned about the endless possible futures. How our lives would unfold later was on my mind, and I speculated we would have grand adventures in the years to come. What mattered at the time was the mere fact we were there together—enjoying being in the now and our smiles without another care in the world.

She felt warm and squirmed as I held her in my arms.

As I think about that instant today, I know I must have been wondering whether I would always be able to provide the emotional support she would need. The only help she needed that day was a simple smile and reassuring hug. My feelings were unconditional. I wanted nothing but the best for her. I was on an emotional roller coaster–new feelings like nothing I had ever experienced. Unconsciously, I also must have known someday, someone else would take my place.

None of that mattered. All that mattered was the complete filling of my heart and the feelings of satisfaction, joy, and exhilaration. Her crooked smile said it all. It was a moment I have never forgotten. A story I have often told, but not to her. Until now–since I plan to leave this written memory for her to be opened upon my death.

When I told this story before to others, I marveled at how my daughter could have learned to manipulate me so easily and so soon. The smile did it. Although our relationship was already several months old, it had only been a short while there had been any real communication between us. That morning, from her crib and without uttering a single word, an extremely complex social message had been transmitted, received, and understood. Likewise, she had understood my reaction. I knew as she turned her head and smiled again, she actually realized I knew she could make me react.

She could not have known at the time I would be in her life forever, although someday there would be someone else whom she would turn to. She could not have known both the heartache and the joy that would challenge us in the coming years.

On a distant day in the future, when she called, I would drop everything to be at her side when she needed her father. When I saw her then, many years later, in a hospital bed, my presence was all that was needed again to make her, and me, smile.

An earlier version of "The Power of a Smile" was previously published in Heartbeat, June 2011, p. 13.; Veterans' Voices, 59, No. 3, Fall 2011, p. 15; Love, Sweet to Spicy: A Corrales Writing Group Anthology, Patricia Walkow, ed., North Charleston, SC: CreateSpace, January 2018, pp. 197-198; and Corrales Comment [online], 13 December 2019.

Jim Tritten is a retired Navy carrier pilot living in a semi-rural village in New Mexico with his Danish author/artist wife and four cats.

7

I COULD LOVE YOU... IF YOU LIVE

(BASED ON CHARACTERS AND SETTINGS IN THE BAND IN THE WIND TRILOGY)

WILLIAM JOHN ROSTRON

Her body lay on the gurney, barely clinging to life. *I could love you if you live,* DJ Spinelli thought to himself. He had once written a song that expressed exactly that sentiment. But as she lay there, he knew it wasn't true. He would love her whether she lived or not. It had always been so, and it always would be so—at least since he met her in 1966. However, now three years later, he didn't think she could ever love him. Aylin McAvoy had a greater love than he could not compete with. That addiction was why she was barely clinging to life now.

Why had he never told her? Why had he never done anything at all to let her know of his interest? Sure, he had plenty of excuses, but they all paled in importance as he looked at her possibly taking her last breaths. Yeah, it had been such a long strange trip that had brought the two of them to this point.

It all began when he was sixteen years old and a budding songwriter for a group with unlimited potential. Though he played no instrument himself, the group Those Born Free had asked if they could put music to some poems that he had written. The band held their practices in Jimmy McAvoy's basement, and it was there that he saw Jimmy's sister, Aylin, for the first time. Her auburn hair flowed to the middle of her back and framed her finely sculpted body. Her hair outlined a beautiful face highlighted by blue eyes that sparkled when she smiled, lighting up the room.

However, Aylin was Jimmy Mac's sister, and he was very protective of her. It was an unwritten rule that no one in the band would become involved with her. By extension, that included DJ. He could be involved with the band or make a play for Aylin, but he could not do both. *Would she even be interested?* It all became real at one of the band's practices.

"Don't even think about it," whispered Johnny, DJ's friend who had introduced him to the band.

"Think of what?" replied DJ in an equally conspiratorial tone.

"Aylin. I saw you looking at her ass as she walked up the stairs."

"I don't know what the hell you're talking about."

"Bullshit, DJ, you were practically undressing her with your eyes. What were you thinking?"

"Johnny, I think I like her. I mean, really, really like her."

· · ·

"And I think you're freakin' nuts."

"I won't do anything about it because of the band, but that's how I feel."

"Damn, DJ, you're either lying to me, or you're more freakin' stupid than I thought. I know that sure as hell you *are* going to do something!"
　"Why?"

"Because, you idiot, she was looking at you the same way."

DJ never did do anything. A month after their conversation, the whole question became moot. Jimmy Mac and his father had been murdered during a robbery at their family store. The band had broken up. Johnny had told DJ that Aylin had gone into a deep depression. Many nights DJ wished that he had done more to let her know how he felt. If he had, it would not have been awkward for him to call her. Now it was too late. She was gone from his life.
　DJ moved on. He went to Queens College, continuing to work on his prose and poetry writing and launching his own underground music newspaper. He had even taken up the guitar himself and joined a band. Oh, if they could only see him now—Jimmy Mac, Johnny, and the rest of the band...and Aylin.
　In early January of 1969, DJ and his band played at the student center at Queens College. They had played well, and the crowd had even enthusiastically listened to the original songs that DJ had written. Afterward, a small group of his friends approached

him. Most of these guys had known him since they went to high school together only a few miles away. In a commuter college with over 20,000 students, it was essential to have a support group of close friends. However, as most of his inner circle drifted off, one couple stayed with him to talk.

"That was great. We love good rock," blustered Dougie "Douchebag" Wilk. Everyone used the nickname behind his back and even to his face. DJ didn't like him or how he played the system. Dougie had been in college for seven years. He was not stupid—quite the opposite. He probably could have had an excellent GPA if he didn't tend to drop classes during the latter part of each term. Dougie didn't want to graduate. As long as he stayed a student, he couldn't be drafted. Tuition was free at this city college. Dougie incurred no costs while he gamed the system. No one liked what he was doing. He was taking the spot of some other city resident who wanted an education. But here he was talking to DJ like they were best of friends. Something was up.

"That was great. Love that music. We love all music," blustered Dougie. He then turned to the girl occupying his right arm. He kissed her cheek and whispered to her, "Right, doll?" She nodded a very unenthusiastic yes. This was the second reason that Dougie was a "douchebag." He used his exceedingly good looks to bed an excessive amount of college girls. He was the very definition of a love'em and leave'em kind of guy. However, this girl might not even be old enough to be a student at the school. As if Dougie could read DJ's mind, he answered the question.

.   .   .

"This little cutie comes all the way here to the school just to see me."

DJ had finally had it with the whole conversation.

"Well, I know she didn't come here to go to class with you, Dougie. You couldn't even find your way to the freshmen English class you signed up for seven years ago. So Dougie, why are we talking?" The anger had become evident in DJ's voice.

"Calm down, please calm down, DJ, I need to ask you a favor, and I'll make it worth your while. With all your music connections, we were hoping you could hook us up with some tickets to a concert this summer. It's supposed to be the greatest concert ever. I'll give you double the face value for the media tickets that your writing gig gets you?"

"First of all, I have no idea what I'm doing tomorrow, no less this summer. Secondly, Douchebag, I wouldn't do anything for you no matter how much you gave me. So, please just get lost."

"Please," spoke the girl around whom Dougie's arm rested. "Please, DJ."

And DJ knew. He didn't want to know, but he did. This emaciated girl, with sunken cheeks and dullness in her eyes, was Aylin. It had been almost two years since he had last seen her, and the time had not been good to her. Something was wrong. Something was off. It had to be more than depression, and he thought he knew what it was. Caught off guard, he unconsciously continued his conversation just for more time with the girl he had loved.

"So where is this concert, Dougie?"

"Huh," responded Dougie, not knowing what had brought about the change of attitude that had left DJ calling him by his name instead of his nickname.

"I asked where it was."

"Outdoors, on a farm in upstate New York."

"Dougie, I can't promise anything, but I'll look into it." DJ's sudden change of heart had more to do with trying to find out more about Aylin than trying to help Mr. Douchebag. As the couple went to leave, DJ was reminded of the third reason he hated Dougie.

"Thank you, DJ," whispered Aylin as she tenderly gave him a goodbye hug. As her arm slid off DJ's shoulder, he saw them—the tracks of an addict ran down her arm. He said nothing but walked away, fighting back the tears.

. . .

Once the shock wore off, DJ had to decide what he would do. It ate at him day and night before he came to a decision. The Aylin he remembered had been a cheerful, playful, exciting person. She had been full of life. Had the death of her father and only brother taken that all away. DJ tried to understand the depth of her grief. And dammit, that asshole Dougie was taking advantage of this young, fragile girl. He thought to himself that the next time he saw the bastard, he would say or do something he would regret. *Screw that. I'm not going to regret it one bit*, he thought.

In the middle of February, DJ called Mrs. McAvoy and told her he needed to speak with her. All his childhood, DJ had been taught that "snitches get stitches." He knew that Aylin would probably never talk to him again. He could accept that. That is what you did for someone you loved—you sacrificed. In this case, his sacrifice meant that he would probably never see her again.

"I know," was all that Mrs. McAvoy responded to DJ's bad news. Distraught, Mrs. McAvoy felt that she was losing her eldest daughter, and she had no idea what to do. No sooner had she left the room crying than Aylin walked into the kitchen where we had been talking and slapped DJ's face.

"You god-damned snitch," she screamed and buried the nails of her right hand into DJ's face. He did not respond but merely stared outward as she pounded his chest. Finally, when he could take no more of her emotions, he reached out and grabbed both her wrists.

·　·　·

"You may think that Dougie is your boyfriend, but he's using you. He's a selfish prick who could care less about anyone—including you."

All of the fight left Aylin's body, and she stopped struggling with DJ. For the first time in two years, she spoke the truth to someone.

"And I'm using him. He gives me what I need."

"You don't need that shit. You don't, Aylin!"

"DJ, who are you to tell me what I need and don't need. Just because you knew my brother, you think that you can waltz in here and tell me what to do, like...like Jimmy used to do?" With that, the anger stopped, and the tears rolled from her eyes. Her body quivered. DJ released her wrists, and she eased herself to the floor.

"Aylin, it will be okay."

"It won't ever be okay again. I miss Jimmy. I miss my dad.

DJ bent down, and she fell into his arms. As he hugged her tightly, she lost all control of her emotions. She cried uncontrollably—a cry that was long overdue. Drained of emotion, she stayed in his arms, never saying a word. DJ sat silently holding her—never wanting to let go. Eventually, Aylin fell asleep, and DJ tenderly carried her to her bed.

That night DJ Spinelli wrote the most meaningful song of his life. He didn't think he would ever share it with anyone. It was too personal. Yet, the words and the tune came to him in fits of raw feeling. He worked with passion and described what he was going through. When he was done, he played it softly to himself—perhaps the only audience this tune would ever have.

I Could Love You…If You Live
   - DJ Spinelli

I could love you if you live.
   But that doesn't seem to be.
   It's fryin' your brain, drivin' me insane.
   And you're too blind to see.

I could love you, I know it,
   If only you could break free.
   Lines down your arm are doin' you harm.
   Killin' both you and me.

I could love you if you live;
   But that doesn't seem to be.
   Monkey got a hold of your damn soul,
   Chokin' at my heart too, you see.

                     .   .   .

It was 3 a.m. when he put the finishing touches on the song. There was a sadness in facing reality. He was in love with a junkie. What would he do if she chose to love him in return? He didn't know. He just knew that he wanted to be there for her, but he would never accept her self-destruction. He didn't know if he was strong enough to deal with all the baggage that came with Aylin. Yet, he also didn't know if he was deceiving himself when he wrote the final stanza to his song.

I don't think you see,
      what our future could be,
    But I'm not going down all the way,
    ...with you.

Months went by, and DJ would occasionally see Aylin on campus with Dougie. He had decided that there was nothing that he could do to win Aylin. He did not doubt that she was still using the drugs that Dougie gave her. Yet, she did seem a bit more like the girl he remembered from band practices. So maybe she had cut back. At least, that was what he hoped.

Whenever they met, she always had a big hug for him—but it was a hug of friendship and nothing more. DJ knew that what was going on inside her head would remain a mystery to him. Her beauty and her wit beguiled him, yet there was sadness that seemed to overwhelm her soul. But did he still have feelings for her? Did he want to be involved with this troubled, drug-addicted girl? No matter how much he fought it, the answer was yes—If she would have him. However, until she did, he had to live his life and move forward.

As a writer, publisher, and editor of a music newspaper, DJ had started to hear rumblings of the concert that Dougie had referenced. He had a connection with an up and coming solo artist named Chris Delaney. He had never met him in person, but Delaney was a friend of a friend. While interviewing him on a long-distance phone call one night, the singer had revealed that he had been signed for an outdoor concert that summer in upstate New York. DJ began to wonder if perhaps Chris Delaney's career was in a downward spiral. He was calling from some Podunk venue in North Dakota, and now he was scheduled to perform infield filled with cow shit for a few hundred people. *Poor Chris Delaney, his career over before it even started,* thought DJ. *I mean, how do you put on your resume that you performed on some guy named Max Yasgur's farm? And where the hell was Woodstock, New York?*

By July of 1969, DJ realized that perhaps this concert was something more significant than he thought. Delaney had hooked him up with a ticket and a back-stage pass. However, DJ still hadn't decided if he was going. Until…

Neil Armstrong's first words on the moon were greeted with enthusiastic cheers by the crowd gathered in the McAvoy home. After two years of mourning, Adele McAvoy decided that it was time to invite people into her house. It was a small group, but DJ noticed that everyone there had known Jimmy and his father, and not coincidently, it was close to the second anniversary of their deaths. He also observed that Aylin was just a bit too talkative…a fit too flirty…and a bit too high. Though Dougie Douchebag was not there, she had obviously met up with him a bit earlier for a little boost. After all, why should the spacemen be the only ones who were high? DJ's conversation with Aylin would eventually change both their lives.

. . .

"DJ, guess what? Dougie got the two of us tickets to the music concert up in Woodstock."

"Aylin, I don't know if it's going to be as good as you think. Music out there in the middle of a field with no shelter and a few thousand people? Doesn't sound great."

"Dougie says that Credence Clearwater signed up, and so, a lot of groups decided to go too. Besides, he says he has a big surprise for me when the concert ends."

Oh shit! I know what the surprise is, thought DJ but said nothing.

"Yeah, we're going to take my mom's car, and afterward, we're going on a road trip. He won't tell me where. That's the surprise."

"What if your mom doesn't want to lend you her car?"

"Then I'm just going to take it. Dougie says we need the car for the road trip."

Everything he had heard fell together like the pieces of a child's puzzle. He knew that Dougie liked music, but even more than that, he liked his freedom. Rumors on the campus were that the selective service had figured out the douchebag's seven-year college plan's scam. They had started to hassle him. Now he had tickets for Aylin and him. After Woodstock, it was a very short run up the New York Thruway to Canada. DJ didn't care if Dougie went—good riddance. But now, it became apparent that he was taking Aylin.

He had heard Dougie bragging about scoring a large supply of drugs. He now had enough for the concert and a Canadian stash until he found a connection up there. He couldn't allow him to destroy Aylin's life. How long before she would need to do horrible things to keep the money rolling in for drugs? How long before Dougie abandoned her? Who would replace the support she received from her mom and him. He had to watch out for her. But what could he do? Telling her mom hadn't worked out well the first time. But maybe he could do something.

"I'm going too. Maybe we can meet up?"

"How?"

"I got a ticket from a friend."

"Who do you know, Mr. Big Shot?"

"Umm...Chris Delaney." DJ had led her into a carefully laid trap. He had known from previous conversations that the performer he had mentioned was her absolute favorite. She had probably been eight miles high at the time and did not remember the conversation."

"Wow, DJ, you think that I can meet him?"

Hook, line, and sinker thought DJ. "Yes, of course, we'll meet up as soon as I get there. You just stay to the left side of the stage. We'll watch Chris perform, and then I'll take you and..." DJ knew he didn't want to call him "Douchebag" while in Aylin's house. However, even saying "Dougie" put the distinct taste of vomit in his mouth."

"Dougie," finished Aylin, thinking that DJ had merely forgotten his name.

"Yeah, I'll meet you *two*," DJ spat out. "I mean, with a few thousand people there, you shouldn't be hard to find."

"DJ, I think that they have sold more tickets than you think."

"C'mon, what'd they sell 4,000? I mean, your brother played in front of that many people in Central Park." DJ realized that bringing up her deceased brother, Jimmy Mac, was never a good mood builder, and they both stood quietly and watched the coverage of the moonwalk.

DJ could not know that as Neil Armstrong took his first steps on the lunar surface, 186,000 tickets had already been sold. By the day and time the first act performed a month later, an estimated half-million people were in attendance. Tickets became useless, and the area was overwhelmed by the crowd. On late Friday night, when the New York Thruway was shutdown, DJ realized that he would have to sleep in his car that night and trek the last twenty miles to the venue the next day.

Exhausted from a night of sleeping in an uncomfortable car, he arrived at the staging area in time to see the obscure band Quill perform "They Live the Life." DJ looked over the sea of humanity and thought, *how true, how true.* He immediately realized that any hope of finding Aylin before their Sunday rendezvous was hopeless. Using the press credentials that Delaney had obtained for him, he had worked himself into a relatively good location to view the performers. Careful to make his water and food last, he relaxed and enjoyed the music. He never stopped scanning the crowd in hopes of spotting Aylin. Before leaving home, he spoke to Mrs. Mac and knew that Aylin had taken her car—without permission. Somewhere on the fringes of this chaos sat the getaway car for a Canadian adventure. DJ had to find her. Life in Canada with "Douchebag Dougie" would destroy Aylin.

Aylin and Dougie had been among the first group to arrive at the festival. They had prime seats in front of the stage. However, neither of them had heard very much of the music presented. Dougie had brought enough drugs to last them through not only the three days of the festival but also into his first week or two in

Canada. Dougie's brush with academics had not gone well, and the selective service had scheduled his physical for August 21. He was not going to show up. He decided on a quick concert, and then Canada awaited. Assuming it would take at least a week to establish a dealer in his new homeland, the supply he brought would ensure an unbroken succession of highs on both sides of the border. However, at the actual rate they were both consuming his stash, they might not have that luxury. They had already gone through the weekend's allotment and were well into the Canadian portion of his supply. They did not seem to know or care about this fact.

Chris Delaney was scheduled to go on after Joe Cocker on Sunday afternoon. Midway through the Cocker's performance of "Feelin' Alright," DJ started to work his way toward the stage entrance where he had arranged to meet Delaney and Aylin. Dark clouds consumed the skies, and a pending storm became obvious.

Dougie had never intended to take Aylin with him to Canada. He just was not interested in her enough to make her part of his new life. Yet, he did need her car to finish his journey, and he intended to leave while she was stoned. The scheduled meeting with Chris Delaney was a perfect opportunity to sneak away. As they worked their way to the stage, Dougie suggested a brief stop to take the edge off. As he injected Aylin vein in her left arm with a high dose of heroin, he couldn't know that only minutes before she had injected her right arm. As they continued toward her long-awaited meeting with Delaney, Aylin's body started to feel the effects of the double dose of drugs, and the world spun in her eyes. The first time that DJ saw Aylin was to witness her total physical collapse. The woman he loved was plunging face-first into the mud ten yards away from him. Next to her stood the frightened Dougie, who was obviously in the throes of panic.

"I don't know her, but I just saw her take a lot of drugs," babbled Dougie, failing in his excitement to even recognize DJ.

"Which drugs? What did she take?" yelled DJ as Dougie started escaping through the crowd. He saw the love of his life fading in and out of consciousness and was confused. He knew that Aylin desperately needed help, but he also knew that a doctor would need to know what she had taken--and only Dougie could answer that question.

DJ pleaded with the crowd around him to stop Dougie's escape. He would chase the escaping bastard if someone else brought this girl to the clinic. Stoned faces stared at him blankly as his eyes kept rotating from Aylin to the fleeing Dougie. "A Little Help from My Friends" could be heard in the background as Joe Cocker's set was coming to an end. *That's just what I need right now is a little help from friends, strangers—anyone* thought DJ. He weighed his choices, and with a grimace on his face, he waded into the crowd. As Aylin lay unconscious, he caught up to Dougie just as the first thunderclap enveloped the crowd, and torrential rain began.

"What did she take?" screamed DJ to be heard over the screaming crowd and the thunder.

· · ·

"I don't know what you are talking about?"

DJ right fist landed on Dougie's jaw and sent him sprawling in the mud.

"I don't have time for this shit, Dougie." He bent down and grabbed his collar and pulled his face so close that Dougie looked aside. "Do you hear me?" He body-slammed Dougie to the ground."

Dougie told DJ what he wanted to know. His face wet with both tears and rain, DJ started to head back to Aylin. After two steps, however, he turned around to his victim.

"Give me the keys to Mrs. Mac's car. I know you must have taken them."

"Who me? Don't know what you are talking about?" whined Dougie, as DJ saw them sticking out of his pants pocket. After he bent down to snatch them, he stood up and gave Dougie a swift kick to the ribs.

"You may still make it to Canada without the car, and you may be able to dodge the draft up there, but..." DJ stopped and kicked him again. As he was walking away, he turned back one last time, "Canada may hide you from the draft, but if Aylin dies, you won't be able to hide from me…ever."

As DJ bent down to pick Aylin up, it seemed like an eternity since he had left her. Her eyelids fluttered, and her breathing grew shallow as DJ kneeled over her.

"Aylin, Aylin, no please," DJ screamed at the still body in front of him. He quickly picked her up in his two arms and started to run toward a medical clinic that had been set up on the premises. Thankfully he had noticed it on his way into the concert the day before. The ear-splitting noise of massive thunderclaps soon drowned out all spoken sounds. The storm that had arrived had put on hold indefinitely any thoughts of music. Within minutes the already saturated ground became inches deep in mud. DJ struggled to see as the rain limited his vision.

"Hold on, Aylin, please . . . please, Aylin, don't leave now," he whispered to her, but his words fell on deaf ears. He could not tell if she was even breathing. DJ soon found himself ankle-deep in mud. As he went to lift his left foot, it stayed mired deep in the muck. With his momentum moving forward and his foot planted, he lost his balance plummeted downward into the sludge. Streaks of lightning filled the sky, and crowds either hugged the ground or ran for what little shelter they could find. With both their bodies encased in thick layers of mud, DJ pushed the dirt away from Aylin's face. He put his ear to her mouth to listen for any sounds of life. There were none. He kneeled over her motionless body, not knowing what to do. In the distance, he heard one stoned concert goer screaming and ignoring the lightning strikes. What was he yelling?

"Don't worry, everyone, this is the age of Aquarius—the sign of water. Enjoy the storm. The gods have sent it to us. Yes, Yes, the Age of Aquarius—a time when we're all *born free*." He then promptly collapsed in the mud but continued to rant. DJ had heard enough.

Born free? Those Born Free? Once when they were on a break at a Those Born Free band practice, Johnny had told him a story about how one of the guys in the band had saved someone's life using something called CPR. Johnny had gone into great detail about how he pushed on his chest and then counted and then pushed again and again. As if in a vision, the actions that Johnny had described to him came back in vivid detail. He put them in some logical order in his mind and then recreated what he remembered on the fallen Aylin.

"I'm not giving up on you. I love you, Aylin," DJ yelled as he pushed and pumped her lifeless body. "C'mon, you can do it." Thunder crashed overhead, and many around him screamed in fear. DJ, however, remained oblivious to his surroundings, concentrating solely on reviving Aylin. Suddenly he felt movement in her body. Her eyes opened briefly and then rolled back in her head. She had started breathing again, but it was weak strained breathing. He knew he did not have long to get her real help. He rose from the ground to continue his journey toward the clinic.

. . .

The fields that only minutes before had been alive with crazed concert-goers were now a sea of bodies attempting to become one with the Earth in order not to be hit by the rapidly striking bolts of electricity from the sky. Only one figure now stood upright as he trudged forward, constantly moving his eyes between the path before him and Aylin's face. As he reached an incline in the ground, the going became more difficult. He would lose his footing and fall every few steps, always careful to protect Aylin from the impact. His legs weakened, and it was only his feeling for her that kept him going. Ten feet from the peak of the hill, he fell a final time. If he could just get up once more, the clinic was in eyesight. He could make if he could stand, but legs had not the strength to rise. He tried over and over again. Again, he felt her heartbeat fade and had to use CPR again, and this time he used mouth-to-mouth resuscitation that he had once learned in health class. As she started to breathe more normally, DJ smiled and merely stared at her face. He again lowered his lips to hers. Not resuscitation—but rather a kiss. Briefly, Aylin opened her eyes and looked at him.

"Goddamit! Get up, you piece of shit," he yelled at his own fatigued body. Yet, his body answered with only rejection of his pleas. She did not have long. He thought of those pleading blues eyes that just stared at him. He had to do it. Kneeling in the mud, he inched forward...five feet...ten feet. He thought he saw someone through the rain.

Nurses took Aylin from DJ's arms and ushered them both into the clinic.

"Can you help her?" DJ screamed.

"What did she take?"

DJ explained her double dose of heroin, and the nurse explained that a doctor might be able to help her.

"And I'm guessing that there is none here."

"You don't know how lucky your friend is. Dr. Lopez made a trip here to deliver a baby. Do you believe this shit? Coming here nine months pregnant. Anyway, I'll tell her to see your friend...?"

"Aylin, Aylin McAvoy."

Three hours later, Aylin opened her eyes for the first time, and the first sight she saw was DJ.

"Why are you crying?" asked Aylin.

"We almost lost you. Your mother couldn't take that."

"Only my mom? How about you?"

. . .

"I couldn't take that either."

"You know, I did have some moments of consciousness while you were carrying me. I heard some things..." She stopped talking and reached out and held DJ's hand. She looked into his eyes. A slight smile came across her face as she spoke.

"You know, it was weird...out there in the field, I seem to remember your mouth on mine. Were you getting fresh with me?"

"No, no, that was mouth to ..."

She stopped him. "I know what it was. DJ, I been thinking while I've been laying here. I know what you have been trying to say to me. Jimmy Mac wouldn't have wanted me to throw my life away. I know that this is killing my mother... and you. I've made a deci-sion. I'm going away to rehab."

"Good." was all that DJ could think to respond.

"And DJ, will you wait for me? It's too much for me to expect, but it's not too much for me to ask.

"Aylin, I could love you...I mean...I do love you."

. . .

"And, DJ, when I come back from rehab, I want our second kiss to be a hell of a lot better than that first one."

William John Rostron

The author recently completed a trilogy of novels steeped in the late 20th and early 21st centuries' music and culture. *Band in the Wind, Sound of Redemption*, and *Brotherhood of Forever* have received critical acclaim from Writers Digest, the Online Book Club Review, and many other reviewers. These books have found readership on four continents (North America, Europe, Australia, and Asia).

In the past, he has published over two dozen non-fiction articles in newspapers and magazines. These writings included four full-page op-eds in New York Newsday. He was also presented an award by Nelson DeMille for his historical fiction short story, "The Last Artifact." Recently, his short pieces have in published in nine Red Penguin anthologies:

Three of his short pieces were accepted into the Visible Ink anthologies in 2018, 2019, and 2020. Each year, a dozen works are chosen for reading and presentation on stage in New York City. In 2018, "Pretty Flamingo" was given this honor. As an encore, "In the Garden of Eden" was performed in 2019. In 2020, his short work "Ava's Bubble" was read by Tony and Emmy nominee Victor Garber on a nationally televised streaming show. All of these are available for viewing on www.williamjohnrostron.com.

In his previous career, the author instructed students from the ages of 9 to 90. In his life, he taught elementary school, middle school, high school, college, adult education, and teacher training. He holds degrees from Queens College, Stony Brook University, and Long Island University.

Born and raised in Queens, NY, William John Rostron now splits his time between his home on Long Island and traveling the country in his Tiffin motorhome. When not writing, he is busy completing a bucket list of travel adventures. In the past 16 years, he and his wife Marilyn have traveled 120,000 miles. These journeys have taken them to the 48 contiguous states, 133 national parks, all 30 major league baseball stadiums, 154 cities and towns, two Canadian provinces, and a variety of unusual experiences and locations. Many of these locations have served as backgrounds for his books.

He presently working on a novel, *Lost in the Wind*, and an anthology, *A Flamingo Under the Carousel*.

www.WilliamJohnRostron.com

8

———

THE WRITING WAS ON THE WALL

STEVE DEWOLFE

Steve: October 10, 1964. ...even before we met. The wall was at the back of the left-field bleachers at Yankee Stadium in Game 5 of the 1964 World Series. The words were "PUT IT HERE, MICK" (for Mickey Mantle), written in huge black letters on a bedsheet and attached to the wall on billboard nail pops. My three friends and I received lots of cheers for the sign, but, shortly before the game began, the Stadium staff took the sign down. There were a lot of boos. "The Mick" later won the game, 2-1, with a home run.

Luann: I was there, in first base box seats with my father. We always came early to catch batting practice. My father spotted the sign on the bleacher wall and pointed it out to me, the one with the crush on Mickey. I cheered the sign and booed the attendants who removed it, along with everyone else.

· · ·

Steve: October, 1965. College choice time. Having received offers from several colleges, I started the process of long walks and talks with parents and friends, narrowing the choices to Manhattan College and Fordham University. I was leaning towards Manhattan, but my best friend decided on Fordham. I changed my mind; Fordham it was....

Luann: College choice made, my family alma mater, Indiana University. I even had my dorm assignment. Then came the fateful letter, awarding a New York state scholarship that my parents insisted I accept. The only New York state school I had applied to, Fordham University, became my new home for four years.

Steve: October 11, 1968. One month earlier, as juniors, I had noticed Luann on the rifle range at Fordham University. I had joined the men's team; she was on the women's. She was always beautiful, but she was something else in shooting garb–and when shooting. This particular Friday night, the men had a home match against another school. I was sitting with some teammates in a small eating area when Luann came in, got some coffee, and looked for a place to sit. For some reason beyond mere manners, I got up the gumption to pull out a chair next to me and ask "Why don't you sit here?" When she did, I felt happier than for any bulls-eye I had shot that night!

Luann: I had joined the rifle team as a favor to a dorm mate. It was the first varsity sport for women on what, until three years ago, had been an all-male campus. She insisted that it needed our support; I agreed. During the joint practices, I noticed but ignored the men's team members. I was already engaged to a senior. Until I wasn't. I cried for three days, then washed my face, got dressed, and went to join my teammates supporting the men in their first home match. I got my coffee, came to the table and someone pulled out a chair for me and asked me to "sit here". I saw a handsome face, a pair of very blue eyes, and a kind smile. I sat down, and the writing was on the wall.

Steve: Winter, 1968-1969: Our friendship deepened, and I made a remarkable discovery. I had asked Luann what *she* considered—not for the first time, and certainly not for the last time—a dumb question, and she responded "Why? Because I love you, you fool." I don't remember the question, but I'll never forget her response, and she was right—not for the first time, and, OK, certainly not for the last time—she did love me, and I guess the writing was on the wall. I've been a fool for love ever since.

Luann: We finished each other's sentences, we liked so many of the same things, we had long discussions about the life we wanted to live together, and our differences enriched us and opened new vistas. We could see no future that did not include each other.

Steve: November 8, 1969. Senior year, we decided to marry and completed the arrangements in a month. We were married on a glorious autumn afternoon that followed three days of torrential rains at the back end of a hurricane. We skipped graduation the next May to go on our honeymoon.

·   ·   ·

Luann: Marrying was an impulsive decision. Our families were shocked and apprehensive, convinced we were too young. We were so young that Steve, not yet 21, had to have his parent's permission to marry. I was over 18 and, in the state of New York at that time, women over 18 were considered adults. It wasn't until Steve's birthday party three weeks later that my father-in-law informed me that, for the past three weeks, I had been my husband's legal guardian. All that power... and I didn't know until it was too late!

Steve: The New York Times, November, 1969, reported as a human interest story that the senior captain of the Fordham University men's rifle team, Stephen deWolfe, and the senior captain of the Fordham University women's rifle team, Luann Speciale, had been married on November 8th in the University chapel...

Luann: We have spent the next four decades raising five children and living that life we had discussed at such length all those afternoons ago. One day, in casual conversation, I was comparing teenage girls having crushes on Derek Jeter and the crush I had on "The Mick", "I remember his last World Series", I said. "There was this great homemade sign in the bleachers that was my favorite of all, it said–"

Steve: "Put it here, Mick!" Wow! Talk about Kismet! We still finish each other's sentences, and the writing is still on the wall. For our fortieth, or Ruby, anniversary last fall, I completed a cross-stitch card and enclosed the poem I wrote for the occasion:

·   ·   ·

Four decades since our love took off like a rocket,
    I've made you this card in the shape of a locket
    With shiny, deep red color to commemorate
    Forty yearly flights we've completed to date.

We grew up in Brooklyn, but our paths never crossed
    Until into Fordham's melting pot we were tossed.
    We've never been rich, but to count all our riches
    Would be as hard as counting this card's cross-stitches.

We've been a crew of two, your husband and my wife,
    In flights 'round planet Earth and through universe Life.
    While most flights have let us enjoy each day and night,
    Others needed all our skills to maintain safe flight.

Some flights have been journeys where new vistas abound,
    But even when we've orbited familiar ground,
    Apogees and perigees of varying height
    Provided different perspectives on every flight.

It's been a constant for us: in all that we've seen,
    Our desire to teach has remained just as keen.
    We've shared what we've gleaned from our flights' trove of
treasure
    So, on their own flights, others gain as much pleasure.

While forty flights is deemed a Ruby occasion,

I offer a gift of a different persuasion:
Five children, from whom our pride and enjoyment stem;
Together, they form a necklace: each one a gem!

There's a growing group at each launch and landing,
    With their smiles, applause, cheers, or ovations standing.
    Through the new flights we'll take and light-years we'll
    travel,
    May this card's stitches – and we – never unravel.

While we have alternated our telling of our story, whether the writing is on the wall or on the card, it's safe to say that neither of us wants the last word.

A five-decade IT professional by trade, Steve deWolfe has been writing poetry for more than 30 years. His subjects include life, love, and sports, and his rhymes have sometimes taken an unusual point of view. His baseball poem "Final Flight", from the point of view of the baseball itself, was accepted by the National Baseball Hall of Fame. His works have appeared in three earlier *Red Penguin Collection* anthologies. As a husband, father and grandfather, the scope of his writings and poetry will continuously expand.

Steve can be reached at steve.dewolfe@gmail.com.

9

THEN I SAW HER FACE

ELLA MOON

— Highway in the middle of nowhere, 2:33am

"Sand in my shoes, sand in my shoes" Jamie sings tunelessly, scuffing her feet and staring out the window.

They're the only car on the road, have been for miles, so Sam feels safe turning her gaze to Jamie for a moment. The lights by the side of the highway illuminate her ginger curls in flashes of brilliance.

"Well, that's what you get for wearing your shoes onto a beach. Who does that?"

"We'd never been to that beach before, I didn't want to accidentally wind up with a needle in my foot."

"We *did* look it up first. I feel like someone on Google Reviews might have mentioned if it was a common diabetic-junkie garbage bin."

"You can never be too careful," Jamie tells her solemnly, gaze still on the side of the road whizzing by. "Speaking of which, I know you're looking at me. Watch the road, Chan."

"Whatever you say, O'Reilly."

– Still the middle of nowhere, 2:54am

A wispy stream of cloud floats across the crescent moon, and stars peek out here and there from their fluffy coverings. Jamie is dozing with her head against the window and their black-and-silver blanket wrapped around her. It's come free at her shoulder, and Sam reaches out with one hand and tucks it back under. Jamie murmurs her name, then falls silent again.

The oldies station is playing softly on the radio. Sam recognises the song because it's one of Jamie's favourites – The Monkees, 'I'm A Believer'. Sam may be a believer, but she's rapidly becoming certain that she's also a coward. The two of them could have just flown across the country to their friend's wedding, but Sam had suggested they road trip – she'd told Jamie that they could both use the quiet time, which was true, but she'd had plans of her own. On a road trip together to a wedding should be the perfect time to tell your best friend that you're in love with her, right? But every time she opened her mouth the words got swamped underneath a wave of anxiety, and she just stopped talking. And every time she cursed herself roundly for it.

She's supposed to be the bravest person Jamie knows, but it's their last night on the road and these things always seem so much easier in the midnight hours, and cursing had yet to help her.

– Maybe the middle of somewhere, 3:27am

. . .

Jamie sees the neon drive-through lights before Sam does, and pats her on the shoulder, pointing to it up ahead.

"We should switch, and I could use a cup of coffee," she tells her.

Sam nods and puts the turn signal on. As they pull in, her stomach grumbles loudly and she finally registers what her body has probably been trying to tell her for the last hour. "Oh my god, I'm starving."

"You finally going to crack and order fast food in my presence?"

"It's not just in your presence," Sam objects. "I never order fast food. Mama would kill me."

"I won't tell her if you don't."

"You know you crumble the moment she looks in your direction."

Jamie laughs. "I'm sorry, she's intimidating! You know my mum's a softie, I have no immunity built up to those steely-eyed glares!"

An exhausted-looking woman in a hastily jammed on black cap approaches the screen. Sam seizes the opportunity to get in the last word. "You met my mother when you were eleven, that's plenty of time to build immunity. You just can't hold up under pressure."

Jamie scats the opening to the Queen song as Sam turns to the drive-through employee. "Could we get one large black coffee, one small Coke, and a cheeseburger and fries? Thanks."

The woman nods. Before Jamie can open her mouth, Sam tells her, "Yes, you can have some of my fries."

"Good, because I was going to take them anyway."

. . .

— Drive-through in the middle of nowhere, 3:52am

"Okay, how long can it take to package a cheeseburger?"

"I mean, she's probably the only employee back there. Maybe she's making it from scratch," Jamie suggests.

"What, killing the cow and everything?"

"Maybe," Jamie starts, with that tone that means she's about to go off on a wild tangent, "maybe it's my coffee that's causing all the trouble. Maybe the coffee machine has come to life, and it's finally taking its revenge for a lifetime of oppression and bad beans. Maybe she's in there right now being held down by the milk frother while it turns her arms into spouts." Sam tries not to be too obvious about the love on her face, watching Jamie's hands fly around as she tells her dramatic envisioning of the delay. "Wouldn't we hear her screaming?" she asks.

"No, the deep-fryer is gagging her. There's a whole kitchen appliance revolt going on back there."

"Ah." In the centre well between them, there's a small pile of seashells gathered from the needle-less beach. Sam picks one up and rolls it around, noting how the glaring neon light of the drive-through sign glints off it at sharp angles. It's a masterful distraction, really, until she looks up and sees Jamie watching her, a knowing smile resting in her eyes.

"Are you ever going to say it?" she asks with gentle curiosity.

"Say what?" The shell is cool against her hand, which feels suddenly hot.

"What you came on this trip to say."

"Why do you think I came on this trip to say anything?"

"I've known you since we were eleven, as you reminded me earlier."

"You mean when we placed our orders? Pretty sure we *were*

eleven then. Either that or we're a hundred and eleven now," Sam quips, but Jamie just keeps watching her, gaze level.

"If you won't say it, I will."

Sam's breath stutters.

"I love you, Sam." Jamie's green eyes are wide and honest, and her voice has layered echoes that Sam's never heard before.

— Drive-through in the middle of nowhere, 4:01am

Sam kisses Jamie.

Jamie kisses back.

"Order up!" calls the woman behind the screen.

Ella Moon is actually three writers stacked on top of each other wearing a trenchcoat. The one on top writes sci-fi and romance, the one in the middle writes literary drama, and the one on the bottom spends its time making outlandish quantities of tea and trying to convince the other two that they don't really need to be writing right this moment. Together, they have stories published in '72 Hours of Insanity: Writer's Games' Vol. 7 & 9, online at Little Old Lady Comedy, Defenestration, and CommuterLit, and upcoming in Crimeucopia's 'Cosy Nostra' anthology. One or the other of them can at most times be found ignoring the advice of the other two and trying to buy more books and/or mugs and/or sweaters.

10

SOMEBODY'S UNICORN

SHEVAUN CAVANAUGH KASTL

When I was a child there was a movie called "The Last Unicorn." I was really young, probably six or seven when I saw it, so my memory is dim at best. It was based on a book I think, but I only remember the movie. I was completely enthralled by the fantastical tale of a beautiful, talking unicorn, the last of her kind, who embarks on a quest to discover what happened to the rest of her species and bring them all back from the ends of the earth.

I only recall brief scenes of the film–images, really: the brave unicorn leaving the forest of perpetual summer, her capture by an evil witch who puts her in a cage, a clumsy magician who spells her into human form to save her, a castle set high on a cliff overlooking an angry sea, and a handsome prince with whom she falls in love whilst in human form.

I have the distinct recollection of watching the movie with my childhood playmate Megan. Megan didn't really like the film. I'll admit it was kind of dark, even a little creepy. But she *really* didn't like the ending. You see, Megan was all about the Prince and the Unicorn. She *loved* the love story. Forget the triumph of good over evil or the hero's journey. I, on the other hand, was all about the Unicorn's epic quest. Her courageous answer to a calling far greater than herself. Her *destiny*.

** SPOILER ALERT **

The Unicorn and the Prince do not live *Happily Ever After*.

Sorry, Megan.

Long story short, the Unicorn defeats an Evil King (incidentally the Prince's father) who drove all the other Unicorns out into the angry sea. When she kills the King, they are set free and return with the incoming tide. She bids her loving Prince farewell. He is sad, of course, and so is she. After all, accepting one's destiny involves sacrifice. Being a hero isn't supposed to be easy! In the end, she asks the clumsy Magician to spell her back to her true form so that she may return to the enchanted forest with the rest of her kind.

Yep, it's all coming back to me. This is sorta what I recall after the credits rolled...

Megan, "That wasn't good. They were supposed to get married!"

Me, "No they weren't! She was on a quest!"

"But they were in loooove!"

.   .   .

"That doesn't matter."

"But the Prince!"

"He's fine. He'll live."

Megan, now whimpering, "Nooooooo!!!! She *said* I love you!"

Me, growing frustrated, puffing out air, "She loved him! Ok? But sometimes... there are all... there are... a lot of different kinds of love, ya know?"

"Noooo. I mean, what do you mean?"

My little six-year-old brain was hard at work, trying to summon the right words to make Megan understand what was so *obvious* to me.

The Unicorn had a purpose and it wasn't an engagement.

Megan huffed and puffed and stomped her feet in protest. "They were in love and they should get married! If you love some-body, you marry them, and then, you have a baby!"

That did it.

I fired back "You're wrong!" *Even at six, I had the courage of my convictions.*

But, as Megan continued to push back with impassioned pleas of "But Whyeee???", I found that words had failed me.

· · ·

"Because... because... (exasperated sigh) She's a *Unicorn!*"

I couldn't make Megan understand. And I couldn't quite explain it myself... that I preferred for the Unicorn to stay true to her identity and go on to undoubtedly another magical adventure, alone, but exalted.

This, of course, was about seven years prior to Disney's adaptation of *The Little Mermaid*. I'm sure Megan was thrilled when Ariel gave up her fishtail for feet and the love of a Prince named Eric.

It's not that I don't like a good love story. Hell, I was a Disney Princess! LITERALLY.

More on that later.

I've just always seen romantic love as... well... like a scene in a snow globe. This lovely image of *Happily Ever After* enclosed in a sphere of glass. And I'm outside, looking in. I've never been able to truly picture a life with someone. Never been a part of that scene in the globe. And it never really bothered me. I was always on an adventure. Always seeking ways to make an imprint on this world, to do something remarkable. I suppose I was always on a quest. And love–the whole "I do" and white-picket-fence thing–just never really cut it. I got close once, but it was a disaster and left scars that will probably never fully heal. Maybe I'm scared, guarding my heart like it's made of glass. The thought of investing my whole self in another human being might shatter it to pieces if I choose poorly. I don't know.

I don't think so though. I have loved, at varying degrees anyway. I will love again. I think perhaps I simply prefer to be a

Unicorn. I guess that's why I've only had a handful of relationships. I never fully committed. There was always something wild and unattainable about me. Most of the men who have claimed to love me were possessive. They weren't all bad or anything, but I think my free spirit was alluring to them because it could never be wrangled. I don't know how I feel about that actually. A little sad maybe, because these days, I'm starting to get the feeling that I'm going to grow old alone.

I'm not saying this to be a downer. It's a distinct possibility is all. Maybe what's in my heart is simply too big for any one person. And No, I didn't mean that as a slight against monogamy. I am a one-man kinda gal. But maybe the scope of my emotions transcends the glass globe. And serves a higher purpose.

In any case, you're probably wondering why I got on this whole tangent in the first place and what in the hell do mythic creatures and a thirty-five-year-old movie matter today? You know how there is that one person who holds a special place in your heart? They're not the one that got away. They're not *the one*... but they hold a piece of you. And you hold a piece of them. They are a living, breathing moment in time that has long since passed, that you bottle up and keep with you. They're a song on the radio. They're a scent carried by the breeze. A whispered sound or a word you've committed to memory that will always be lovely.

His name is David and he called me today.

It's been more than a decade since we last spoke and he's married now and lives on the other side of the country. I don't know why exactly he called. We didn't speak long. He confessed to being drunk which made me sad. In any case, he said three words that pierced my heart. The same three words he said once before, nearly twenty years ago. "You're my Unicorn."

I remember that night back in college. I was leaving. My freshman year hadn't even ended when I was cast as Cinderella in a new musical Disney was doing on board their new cruise line. He wanted me to say I'd come back to him. He wanted me to say we would be more than friends. He wanted me to say "I love you."

I didn't.

That's when it happened. At night, outside of Flather Hall, David bid me farewell with a heavy sigh and three words. "You're my Unicorn." At the time I remember feeling giddy and self-important, high on the notion that anyone would say such a thing to me, about me, even if I didn't feel the same. I was so young, and a little insensitive. Especially since I had never felt the gravity of the feelings that come with being in love.

Now, all these years later, I was hearing the words spoken again. There was a long silence on the phone as I considered how to respond now. I couldn't really think of anything else to say other than "I'm sorry." Another moment of silence. I don't know what I was expecting to hear, but he simply said. "It's ok. I just wanted you to know. You're wild and fierce and noble and sometimes, you're a disaster, but you're just the best."

I ended the conversation shortly after with an excuse that he may or may not have believed. It just wasn't an appropriate conversation to have. But I've been thinking about it all day long. And for some reason, I remembered that movie.

And I understand now what I couldn't adequately explain to Megan all those years ago. Love is a part of every story, but it's up to each one of us to decide how we choose to define it. For some people, love is another person and that person is the be-all, end-all. And that's a beautiful thing. For others, it's the pursuit of something extraordinary that has yet to manifest, and the promise of what might be shines like a beacon in the dark for the lonesome traveler.

But the rarest form of love is when someone sees you for exactly who you are and is willing to let you go *be you*, even if it's without them, even if it doesn't make sense, even if it hurts.

At the end of the movie, the Prince was okay. He got to love a Unicorn. And I'd like to think that he went on to find another Mortal to love and live Happily Ever After.

As for the Unicorn...

She journeyed on, not away from love, but toward it, because of it, and far better for it.

Shevaun Cavanaugh Kastl is a natural-born Storyteller. While she began as a Singer and Dancer in such professional NY stage productions as On the Town, Disney's Beauty and the Beast, and West Side Story, Shevaun later discovered her true passion - Writing and Filmmaking. Her first Short film, Conversations With Lucifer was honored among hundreds as one of four films to screen at the historic Grauman's Egyptian Theatre. Her second script, The Mourning Hour, won the title of Best Screenplay at the Slugline International Short Screenplay Competition and the film went on to receive critical acclaim with top honors at The Grand Off Film Festival in Warsaw, Poland, among many other festivals.

While Shevaun continues to write for the Big Screen, she has expanded her literary portfolio to include Poetic Prose, Short Stories, Anthologies and One-Act Plays. She has now written three Feature Screenplays and is currently writing a Psychological Thriller as well as a Fantasy Novel.

11

UNREQUITED IN THE PARK: APHRODITE WITH A SALAD

DAVID LANGE

Bryant Park, New York City. The year is irrelevant. I suppose it was probably a couple of years ago, now. I do recall that it was a lovely spring day. Do my eyes betray me? Perhaps I should start over. I know exactly when it was. It was just after 2pm, on June 25th, 2018. She was Aphrodite with a salad. She reminded me of many things I had forgotten about love. We never spoke.

In search of an apartment to position myself near a job that I would eventually be offered... and ultimately turn down, my brother and I had spent the better part of the morning and early afternoon wandering about Manhattan, looking at potential residences on my list. A former messenger in Manhattan, there was no one I trusted more to provide insights on neighborhoods, travel challenges, and places to rest. And it was definitely time to rest. With tired feet, we arrived at the beautiful Bryant Park. I'd been by there many times, primarily on trips to and from the New York Public Library, but had never found a reason to stop. Part of the park is built above the vast underground archives of the Library.

The lovely 9.6-acre patch of green, amidst a sea of concrete and steel, featured a fair amount of outdoor seating, walkways, and beautiful gardens. It was the perfect place to catch our breath and continue our conversations about life.

My brother and I settled at a small table, benefitting from the shade provided by several trees. We sat; we talked; we watched people. That's when Aphrodite descended from the sapphire blue sky and took up her rightful position upon a glistening golden throne. The world about her, to my astonishment, seemed unaffected. People continued to walk by and the pigeons carried on with their scavenging efforts. Perhaps if she had arrived upon her jewel-encrusted chariot, borne forth by a team of ivory-white doves and heralded by the trumpet fanfare of a thousand angels, those around me might have been as wonderstruck as I. My brother might have noticed her, too. As it was, the goddess radiating with celestial glory a mere twenty feet behind him, my brother was woefully unaware of the divine presence nor the reason his brother's gaze drifted continuously over his left shoulder. My brother spoke and I tried to stay engaged... but I was drifting. No, not merely drifting—I was being swept away by floodwaters carrying my helpless heart towards a sea of bliss; restoring a hope for love that I thought to be long dead within my breast.

Who was she? I wanted to know. She opened the lid to the vessel containing her sustenance and began to eat her salad. I tried, unsuccessfully, not to stare. There was something that drew me towards her like a brilliant sun pulling the orbiting planets ever closer. What was the attraction? It wasn't gravity? Could it be love?

Love or infatuation? I suppose it depends upon your perspective and which dictionary you rely upon to add structure to your thoughts and your descriptions of life's experiences. Sometimes, I prefer to leave words behind and peacefully coexist with my feelings. Maybe that's why I seldom discuss the topic of love. And yet, here I am. And there I was, gazing longingly upon a lovely urban professional on her lunch break. She was pretty but, more so, seemed to have an intelligence about her, and a worldliness. I think that's what grabbed me most. There are beautiful models traipsing all about Manhattan; exotic beauties being photographed in front of every monument and iconic New York backdrop. I acknowledge and appreciate their physical beauty but rarely do I feel inclined to introduce myself and never have I "made a pass" at any. Maybe I should have? I guess I never wanted to be one of the multitudes of male admirers who was constantly grab, grab, grabbing—that must get old very quickly. If I didn't think I would come across as just another guy hitting on them, I might have asked one of these models that very question: "Doesn't that bother you?" I digress. I think smart is sexy. I've always found intelligence to be a critical element of attraction. Kindness, integrity, and a good sense of humor are also major selling points. But these attributes often take time to ascertain. As I considered the stranger transfixing my gaze, my heart was checking boxes well before the interview and evaluation. She had it all. I just knew it. This fetching woman was probably ten years younger than me. Maybe fifteen? Would that be a problem? I didn't think so. Would she? What would she say, should I approach? I desperately scanned the park. I needed a flower vendor to be right over there. The scene played out in my head, again and again, until it was perfected. I would excuse myself from the table. My brother would understand. Brothers are good like that. I'd purchase a single rose —the best of the lot. I would walk over to where Aphrodite sat, consuming her salad, and I would bow as I carefully placed the rose upon her table. "For beauty." That's all I would say. I'd have to get it right. With only two words, this was all going to be about the delivery. But what next? That's the kicker, isn't it. The first date; the first kiss; making love at sunset; the laughs and tears as experiences are shared; the commitment; the legal bonds and rings exchanged; the growing together and evolution of love into something deeper and more meaningful than either partner had ever envisioned possible. That's what I hoped for. Allow me to replay this thought—that is what *"I"* hoped for. *"I, me, my, myself."* A relationship is not about my hopes and dreams. A relationship is about our hopes and dreams. A relationship is caring enough to compromise, and sometimes caring enough to concede. Was I capable of surrendering my dreams? Towards the end of my marriage, I found it increasingly difficult to concede and utterly impossible to communicate regarding such matters. Preserving hope for the future–wasn't that what my divorce was about? Letting go of the dying embers to keep hope alive so that, one day, a fire might burn brightly again? The pain of my divorce had not yet subsided and I was unsure whether I was ready to ignite what little fuel remained about the scarred tissue of my injured heart. Protected behind an imposing stone wall, I had all but thrown away the key to the formidable door that guarded my heart from the death blow that any further onslaught would surely inflict.

"For beauty." This must be about giving and not about receiving. Again, I looked all around, hoping to find a flower vendor; perhaps a florist shop on the perimeter of the park. There had to be something. I would leave the rose and I would turn to walk away. I wanted to acknowledge her presence and to say thank you —you have inspired me. What would she think? What would she say? I wondered. A smile and a thank you? Silence? A rebuke? Would she invite me to sit? If she did, how long should I wait before I asked if my brother might join the meeting? I should ask my brother, shouldn't I? I mean, if this was about giving and not receiving then why shouldn't I introduce Aphrodite to my amazing brother and best friend?

"For beauty." Would my words usher in the beginning of a relationship or expedite the abrupt end of a fumbled attempt to turn an infatuation into something more substantial and enduring. I was ready to buy the flower. My courage was building and I was ready to take that leap. I was ready.

Was this merely a crush? I've had crushes before. Crushes are brief yet intense cases of infatuation for a person who, more often than not, is unattainable. Here I was, dancing about with words off the pages of my dictionary—infatuation, crush, love—where were the boundaries? Was there a natural progression? I wish I knew. I'm sure I could have paid someone well to explain this all to me; and then another to refute what the first psychologist had posited. Where are the darn flowers! What's New York City's fine for picking flowers from a garden?

"For beauty." She was beautiful. She wasn't Aphrodite; she was better. She was of this earth (I think) and she might actually have been attainable, in so much as any person can be "attained." There was hope that a relationship might blossom. She looked smart and worldly and very lovely in the beautiful way that mortals do, far from the columned porticos of Mount Olympus.

I looked, once more, towards the gardens. And I considered the entirety of the scene as my brother and I pushed back our chairs and stood. City ordinance or not, what right had I to remove a flower from the gardens of Bryant Park? Not all flowers need be picked. Better that some might be left for all to enjoy. Those flowers did not belong to me and I had no right to claim ownership. I turned my eyes towards Aphrodite and I sighed deeply. Not all flowers need be picked.

Was I wrong for not addressing the woman who had captured

my heart for the better part of a half-hour? Perhaps I would have
brightened her day? But then again, I might have caused her
stress? Maybe it was never about right or wrong. On that 25th day
of June, 2018, I chose to leave the garden exactly how I found it.
Nothing moved; nothing changed. But something was moved.
Lock undone, deadbolt slid to the side, the creaking of an impene-
trable oak door within my breast bore witness to a change within
my core psyche. It was Aphrodite that handed me the key to my
heart, a key I had misplaced following my divorce and seldom
considered seeking. I smiled. I looked at the sky and I smiled.
Infatuation, crush, love? It didn't matter, not on this day. What was
important was the feeling within my heart and the glowing
embers of hope, brought to life once more as oxygen poured
through the opening door to my heart. For the first time in years, I
knew that I was capable of love and that I might, someday, learn to
love again. This was a joyous revelation. This was hope. Before
returning my gaze back upon the earthly world below the vastness
of the clear blue sky, I whispered under my breath: "for beauty."
We left the park. I didn't find an apartment that day. I found something better. Love, or at least the hope of love. Either was a
blessing worthy of all my gratitude.

David Lange was born and grew up on Long Island, New York. A
graduate of the United States Air Force Academy, he served for
30 years as an Active Duty officer in the United States Air Force
before retiring in 2018. Colonel Lange is a decorated combat
veteran, and flew numerous combat, combat support, and
humanitarian relief missions during his career. He was awarded
the prestigious Institute of Navigation Superior Achievement

Award in recognition of his life-long accomplishments as a prac-
ticing navigator. David loves sharing stories of hope and inspira-
tion and, in 2020, he published his memoir, *"Quest: My Journey
Through La Mancha."*

www.davidlangequest.com

12

FOUR DAYS OF RAIN

ANITA HASS

"I gotta pick up Susi at her grandma's. Back in an hour. Think you can handle the place on your own that long, Sis?"

Clara cringed. Jorge loved humiliating her, especially when counting on the support of his faithful audience.

"Yeah, sure."

"Yeah? You sure you're sure?" Tomás winked at Jorge and hooted over the blare of the soccer game on TV. Jorge patted his buddy on the shoulder, reached for his jacket and umbrella, and headed for the door.

But all of Tomás's courage evaporated in Jorge's wake. Avoiding Clara's eyes, he paid her for his coffee and slipped out, a promising hush of rain filling his place.

Clara, alone in the bar now, gave a little hop of glee, turned off the TV and heavy metal her brother played from pen drives, and hunted through the small collection of LPs behind the bar. Those, along with the old record player, formed part of the legacy left by their parents from when they opened the place decades before, in Usera, a working-class neighborhood in the south of Madrid.

Embraced by solitude, Clara greeted each frayed and faded record cover; Billie Holiday, Nat King Cole, Dinah Washington... so many friends from a happier time echoing her sad hello.

She chose an album she listened to whenever she was left in peace, one with Helen Merrill and Clifford Brown. She placed the needle on her favorite song, Cole Porter's "You'd Be So Nice to Come Home To", set to loading coffee cups and beer glasses into the tiny dishwasher, and fantasized about what kind of man she would like to come home to, rather than the brother, sister-in-law, and niece she encountered day in and day out.

Sometimes she imagined a northern man, tall and blond, his clear eyes smiling down at her. He would murmur to her in adorably accented Spanish and smuggle her off to his far-away country, where everyone would respect her. At other times he was swarthy, with eyes that penetrated right through to her soul, but loved her nonetheless.

Clara turned on the dishwasher and abandoned her post behind the bar. The space between the tables served as her own personal dance studio. Imagining herself poised and classy, like Helen Merrill herself, she swayed and twirled as she had done years ago, encouraged by her parents and their friends.

A throat cleared behind her. "What?" She spun around, coppery curls flying, her tiny tense frame prepared to confront more of her brother's buddies, full of bumbling questions and excuses to flee.

But it was a real customer, and of the type that rarely frequented their establishment; early forties, dark, smartly dressed, with a kind, intelligent gaze.

Embarrassment paralyzed her but the client smiled. "Helen Merrill. Love that song. I also like Chet Baker's version. Do you know it?"

Clara stared at the recent arrival. She had lived moments like this so many times in her day-dreams. In each version, she piloted the conversation with intelligence and wit. However, now that it was finally happening, she was mute.

There were so many things she could have said; *"Sure I know Chet Baker's version, it's great. I also like the one by Sarah Vaughan, and I love the way Nina Simone sings it! So tragic and tense. But I just can't take the Frank Sinatra version at all!"*

But it might sound pretentious to say those things. And maybe this man was a Sinatra fan. Doubt swelled her tongue and robbed her of the moment forever.

The man hesitated, turned slightly toward the door, and prepared to re-open his umbrella. "You are open, aren't you?"

"Yes, yes. Open. Yes." Self-loathing erupted within Clara and she forced a freakish smile. She struggled to untie her stained apron. How she regretted having let herself go. So many years serving the same old crowd had made her careless. And even that crowd was dwindling, so she had to feel grateful for it.

What was this elegant man doing here, anyway? Couldn't he see this was a dive, reeking of stale beer? At least, ever since her brother had taken over.

"Could I have a gin and tonic, please?"

Gin and tonic. Gin and tonic. When was the last time...? Their usual customers just chugged beer, and from bottles only, because Jorge was too cheap to pay for a new beer tap. And where had he hidden that tattered book of cocktail recipes? The one their mother had used to usher the young Clara through symphonies of flavor before presenting them to her guests with musical reverence.

Cubes of ice fizzed in the glass Clara nudged toward the stranger. He locked her gaze in a wordless thank-you, solemn night-sky hues tinting his hair, eyes, and clothes, and moved off to table three in the corner.

Limp, she began cramming napkins mechanically into holders, watching him. A ragged newspaper, discarded days before, trapped his attention now, passively receiving his firm grip and the gentle graze of his fingers over its surface.

Chips! A distant voice called in her brain. The ideal excuse to go to him. She filled a bowl and moved around the bar, the contents trembling.

"Oh, thank you." He turned slightly. She hovered a moment longer. He looked up, expectantly. She summoned her courage, "How ... how is the gin and tonic?" realizing immediately that he hadn't yet touched it. Her eyes followed the laugh lines which framed his features and punctuated his sun-kissed skin.

"Fine. Thank you. Well..." he chuckled, "I'm sure it is. I haven't tried it yet. You see, I..."

A sudden shriek announced the arrival of her three-year-old niece, Susi, along with Jorge and his wife Yolanda, arguing about a parking ticket, rainwater streaming from their jackets. Clara glanced at the clock. Jorge had said an hour. Barely twenty minutes had passed!

"Ok, Clara, back to work! Stop chatting up the customers." Jorge called out in a big voice.

Yolanda smacked him lightly on the shoulder, "Jorge, *hahaha*, you are so bad! *hahaha*!" Susi copied her mother's laugh. Although she didn't understand the joke, she knew who it was on.

Clara scurried red-faced back behind the bar as her brother approached to greet the new customer. The man raised his glass and took a sip.

"Clara!" Susi pounded her small fist on the bar, "My juice!"

"Here." There was a loud clack of tin against steel as Clara slammed the can in front of her niece. She braced herself for her brother to ridicule her choice of music, the music their parents had woven into the tapestry of their shared childhood. But this time there was no reaction. *"He's a jerk, but not stupid."* Clara thought. Jorge knew it might be wise to cater to this new customer's tastes.

Clara ran a cloth over the bar top. Two of Jorge's friends slunk in, each one cradling a motorcycle helmet under his arm and sporting a soaked black t-shirt shouting out the names of heavy metal bands; Iron Maiden, the first, and ACDC, the second. When they noticed the jazz playing, their eyes leapt from Jorge to Clara, and back again. Jorge shrugged "Got a problem, mates?"

"No, no. None." They stammered.

"Ok, then. What'll it be? Two beers, right?"

At that moment the stranger's chair scraped the linoleum and he stood up, placed a bill of ten euros on the table, and left the bar.

After the door closed, Jorge broke out in loud exaggerated hoots. Iron Maiden and ACDC exchanged glances, then joined in.

Jorge spun around to silence Helen Merrill and replace her with some Rosendo he had downloaded onto the computer.

"What old movie did that guy escape from?" said Iron Maiden between swigs.

"From one with a big budget, judging by the amount of dough he left!" laughed ACDC.

Jorge approached the table, took the ten euros, and handed it to Yolanda, then returned to the bar to hiss in Clara's ear, "I just might toss all this jazz shit out one of these days." She faced him, crushed but not surprised at his sadistic grin. "You don't like the idea, Sis? Well, you're screwed, then, aren't you? I'm the boss now. Mommy and Daddy aren't here to coddle you anymore. You could always look for a job in another bar, although I doubt anyone would hire you."

Clara's head bowed under the hail of snickers from everyone present, including her niece. How she yearned to do just that, escape forever! But where could she go? Who would risk hiring her? Could she do anything else? For thirty-four years these walls had hidden her, first sheltering her, womb-like, with the warmth of her parents, their music, and customers, while she helped out in the kitchen, then at the bar. After school, weekends, holidays. Sometimes they organized jam sessions and begged her mother, a Galician who could easily pass for Portuguese, to sing *bossa nova*.

Clara could never have imagined that, after their parents' deaths, the bar, her haven, would become her hell.

Tuesdays were slow in the best of weather, but when it rained their customers sought refuge in home, take-out pizza, and TV. Clara, on the other hand, welcomed the rain, the tranquility in the bar, the bellow of thunder, the tropical swelter, and freshness. The stench of stale beer surrendered to the perfume of wet earth, and a soft percussion replaced the staccato of TV and angry electric guitars. People connected under an 'us-versus-the-weather' solidarity.

Yolanda wanted little to do with the business, and Jorge usually left Clara alone whenever none of his buddies were around, preferring to run errands and tend to paperwork. She filled the solitude with melodies from her youth, imagining herself outgoing and daring like those jazz singers. She was swaying her hips, holding a spoon for a microphone, and singing "You'd be so nice to come home to" along with Helen Merrill when she heard the now-familiar cough.

"Hello." Monday's stranger smiled at her as he pushed his way through the door.

"Oh..." Clara whirled around, plundering her brain for all the crackling remarks she had been rehearsing for his unlikely return.

"Uh... so, could I have another one of those gin and tonics?"

"Yes... of course." She fled towards the bar, cooled her hands on the ice bucket, and raised them to her cheeks.

As she poured the gin, she tried to think of some brilliant and funny thing to say. *Seems like we have the same taste in music hahaha.* Or *Did you know I invoked you? That's because I'm a witch ...*

No, she wouldn't be able to pull either of those off. She just wasn't the type. If only she were more talkative, like Yolanda, like the Andalusian women she knew, who teased and flirted with bubbling spontaneity. If only she didn't care so much what people thought of her.

She stirred the liquid, taking in his casual elegance. A desperate curiosity seized her; his motivations, his fears; a hundred questions blazed inside. But Clara knew she couldn't hurl herself into profound conversation without the preparatory banter. Her brain raced to construct a coherent sentence.

The bar is usually full at this hour! It's the rain, you know...

Feeling confident, she took a deep breath, turned to hand the stranger his drink, and opened her mouth to present him with her sentence, when the door banged open and in hobbled her elderly neighbor, Benita. "What weather we are having! Oh!" she said, looking left and right, then directly at Clara, "Nobody here?"

Benita was one of those people who invaded a place with her presence. All conversations stepped aside to make room for her.

"Yes, Benita. I'm here." Clara sighed as she placed the stranger's drink on the bar, recognizing his spicy cologne from the day before. She bit her lip, not wanting to sound bitchy in front of him.

"Well, I meant Jorge or Yoli. And where is Susi? Okay, I'll tell you then..."

The man took the glass and headed over to table three. Clara felt an ache deep in her belly and a rush of energy urged her to jump over the bar and go to him. *This may be my only chance!!!* But Benita's presence trapped her.

"I'll have a coffee. Do you remember that smelly tenant in 4D? Well, imagine, the other day ..." and Benita proceeded to jack-hammer Clara with gripes and gossip about the neighbor. Clara nodded respectfully, but could only hear Helen Merrill, now singing "Falling in Love with Love", and she could only see the mysterious customer, the same grimy newspaper lying open on the table in front of him. Rivulets of water formed random trails through the steam on the window behind him, creating a luminous rectangular background for his silhouette.

Just before Benita concluded her story, Jorge pushed open the door, followed by some of his pals.

"Beers for everybody, Clara!" he tapped his keys on the bar and headed directly over to greet the stranger.

"Oh," Benita lit up and turned to the worthier audience. These men were all friends of her son, "Now that you're here..."

Rejected but relieved, Clara began uncapping beer bottles. Jorge was making an uncharacteristic effort of ingratiating himself to the stranger who, smiling politely, left his drink half full, took his umbrella, and abandoned the bar... not, however, without placing a bill of ten euros on the table.

Yolanda was helping Clara clean on Wednesday evening. Clara preferred to work on her own, but she knew she was supposed to show gratitude. Yoli stopped cleaning after half an hour and was busy whatsapping other mothers from Susi's daycare.

"Do you mind if I play some of my dad's old records?"

"Huh? No, I don't care." Yoli was much easier to get along with when Jorge wasn't around.

Clara was floating off the last notes of Billie Holiday's "Don't Explain", and scrubbing a particularly stubborn spot of grease on the window when she felt her favorite Helen Merrill record beckon.

Was Jorge just being mean when he threatened to toss their dad's records? She knew he was capable of it. As she flipped through the dusty album covers, she had the eerie suspicion the collection was shrinking. Her favorite Nina Simone record was gone, as was the Chet Baker album her father had so proudly brought back from a trip to Paris.

The persistent drizzle protected her from the elements, and "You'd Be So Nice to Come Home To" engaged her in a slow dance as Clara dried the glasses she was taking out of the dishwasher. Would he come today? Twice the magic had happened. Could it happen a third time?

Yoli's excited phone conversation with one of the mothers was competing with the record when the door swished open. Today he was wearing a long black raincoat from a 1940s thriller and was struggling to close a large umbrella.

Clara had prepared for this moment. She sported a clean, new apron—mascara framed her green eyes and corrector covered the sad circles under them, but the flock of corny lines she had rehearsed in bed the night before took flight, abandoning her in her prison of shyness.

"Wow! What crazy weather out there!"

"Yes ... uh ... gin and tonic?"

"Ooh, not today, thanks. It's a bit too cold for that. Seems like winter is starting again. What about an Irish coffee? Is that possible?"

"*Mmmmmm*. Irish coffee. My *faaaavorite*." A sexy female voice cooed from the end of the bar. Clara's mouth fell open, then clapped shut. Her sister-in-law was making eyes at him.

"Here, I'll get it for you. Clara, you go and clean up the kitchen." This was absolutely out of order; they had not used the kitchen for more than storage since her mother's death. But the look Yolanda gave her made it clear Clara would have to obey or argue. She chose the less embarrassing option.

Sorting old Tupperware containers, Clara eavesdropped through the little service window behind the bar as her sister-in-law made all the typical small-talk she longed to master herself. Yoli and the stranger chuckled over the weather, found they shared a preference for dark chocolate, and even discovered they both had a distant relative in Teruel. Clara was appalled when Yoli tittered, "Oh, I am so shy! It's embarrassing for me to talk to strangers!"

After ten minutes of chatter, a pack of Jorge's friends filed in. Yoli turned abruptly away from the stranger, changed the music, and began socializing with them. Clara's legs broke into a sprint and propelled her toward the kitchen door, just in time to see the man leave. A bill of ten euros lay on table three.

"Don't you have any errands to run today?" Clara asked Jorge, a bit tensely, the next evening.

"No, I don't, actually. Why?" Jorge smirked at her. "Any reason you don't want me around?"

"No ... I just like to play Dad's records sometimes and I know you don't like them." She felt proud of herself for the quick response.

"Oh yeah? Play Dad's records so that new guy, the fancy dresser, will come in?"

Clara had to admit it. Her brother was evil, but no idiot. She felt her cheeks burn and lowered her head over the sink.

Quite a bit taller than his sister, Jorge was reaching up, placing glasses on the top shelf. He turned to observe her and picked up a knife from the counter. He ran his fingers up and down the blade's edge then tested the point with his thumb. "You know, he comes in every day at seven after work. Whether you play that sappy song or not." He fisted the instrument and grimacing, stabbed the air with each word. "Every day after work he comes here and has a drink before going home for dinner with his wife and kids."

He sneered at her. "How stupid can you get?"

He tossed the knife into the sink and strode off to the kitchen.

Alone and shaking, Clara looked up at the old wall clock. It was ten to seven. How had she never noticed that he always came at the same time? Shoulders slumped, she realized how naive she had been. That little girl fantasy, at her age! She had ached to believe there was some magical force that drew him to the bar, and that she could invoke it by playing *their* song. Despite all the obstacles and intrusions aborting their conversations, she needed to think that deep down there was a reason.

She squinted at her dark reflection in the mirror behind the bar. *A wife and kids. Comes here every day at the same time. Sappy song or not. Straight from the office. Dinner at home. How stupid can you get?*

The record lay waiting on top of the player. She slipped the disk out of its cover, grasped it firmly with both hands, and hissed, *"I never want to hear you again!"* One, *two*, she willed herself, and *snap!* cracked it in two. She tossed the pieces into the garbage. *There!* She turned around and defied the clock. It was five to seven.

Clara stood up, straighter than ever. When the door opened promptly at seven, her heart did not race. It was only some of her brother's pals. It didn't matter, she'd serve them. When she saw her reflection, her face had changed. She looked older, colder. She washed and scrubbed with raging efficiency, one eye on the time. But he didn't come.

Jorge's friends left shortly after eight.

"Well, looks like your boyfriend ain't comin' today." Her brother grinned. "Hey, you didn't really believe what I said before, did you?"

She looked up.

He laughed at the change in her expression and headed toward the kitchen. "It was just a joke, okay? I don't know anything about the guy. No idea if he's married, has kids, where he works, nothing! How would I?"

Clara turned slowly toward the garbage can and knelt in front of it. Vision blurred, she picked up the pieces of broken disk and held them together.

Outside, cars sloshed by, and screeching children splashed through puddles.

From the kitchen came the sound of moving boxes. A moment later, Jorge called to her through the service window, his voice slightly softer than usual.

"*Psst*! Sis, here."

Clara looked up slowly. He was reaching a record album down to her. It was her favorite Nina Simone album with a version of "You'd Be So Nice to Come Home To", the one that had gone missing a while back.

"Try this one."

Anita Haas is a differently-abled Canadian writer and teacher based in Madrid, Spain. She has published books on film, two novelettes, a short story collection, and articles, poems and fiction in both English and Spanish.

Some publications her fiction has appeared in include Falling Star Magazine, The Tulane Review, Literary Brushstrokes, The Zodiac Review, River Poets Journal, Scarlet Leaf Review, Terror House Magazine, Wink and Adelaide Magazine. She spends her free time watching films, and enjoying tapas and flamenco with her writer husband and two cats.

13

THE VIRTUAL GRASS IS ALWAYS GREENER

DEBBIE DE LOUISE

Denise signed into her Facebook account as she did each morning after her children left for school. She saw the red indicator on her message icon displaying five instant messages. She knew whom they were from–her online boyfriend, Pierre. She clicked her mouse over the messages to open them, noting that Pierre's online status indicator was off so they couldn't chat in real-time. She wasn't surprised, as Pierre often slept late or came online at night, despite their five-hour time difference.

All the messages began the same, "Mon amour, Denise." A familiar thrill ran through her body. She figured that's how adulterers felt, but she didn't believe she was cheating. She didn't plan to ever meet Pierre in person. How could she afford a trip to France? And, as a starving artist, Pierre couldn't afford to visit her in New York either.

Denise's boring, computer programmer husband Raymond had no clue she was engaging in a virtual relationship. She'd met Pierre a year ago when she joined a Facebook artists' group. Online Artists was an open group for any professional or amateur artist. She qualified because she taught at a prestigious art school that wealthy parents sent their talentless children to in the hope that junior or Little Me would become another Pablo Picasso or Georgia O'Keefe.

After she posted a few items to the group, Pierre sent her a friendship request. When she accepted, he began to IM her privately. Their discussions about art became more personal, and she learned he was a lonely widower of 45 who couldn't bring himself to seek a woman to replace his lovely Marie who died in a car accident ten years ago. Pierre continued to paint portraits of Marie to keep her in his memory. The ones he sold allowed him to live in their modest apartment near the Eiffel Tower. He displayed the others in his small art gallery or hung them in his house as reminders of his loss.

Denise was fascinated by Pierre's tales of Paris but also saddened by the man and his sorrowful story that she came to know through their lengthy online chats, instant messages, and emails. She also shared with him the monotonous details of her marriage with Raymond. How, after fifteen years and two children, she was left with only her Maine Coon cat, Fred, for affection. It wasn't that Raymond was involved with another woman. He just spent all his time writing computer programs, and their love life was as predictable as programming code.

The kids were no better. Ray, Jr. was 14; Sandy 13. Typical teenagers, they wanted nothing to do with their mother. Denise thought she could find fulfillment at work, but the kids she taught were as snobby as their parents. The only good part of her job was that it was only twenty hours a week, which left plenty of time for her to spend online with Pierre. Through the little French phrases he taught her and his vivid descriptions of Paris, she could live another life. The dishes could sit in the sink and the laundry pile up. The kids never kept their rooms cleaned, anyway, and Raymond was always too preoccupied to notice anything.

Denise continued reading Pierre's messages. All of them were filled with his sweet words and endearments. In the last message, he asked if she would be online that night to chat. He had something important to tell her. Denise knew that Raymond would be in his office working on a program that evening, so she'd be free to work at her own computer in the den. Sandra would be at the movies with a girlfriend and Junior would be at a baseball game.

Throughout the day, Denise's thoughts returned to Pierre and what surprise he might have for her. Her birthday was a week away, and she knew that he'd mentioned buying her a gift. When the package arrived from France, it would be easy to hide from Raymond, since she was the only one who collected the mail.

When she came home from another frustrating afternoon of trying to teach a group of rich brats to paint, Denise tried to keep her mind off Pierre's surprise. She busied herself, making dinner until her daughter walked through the door.

"Hello, Mom," Sandy said. "Can I help you cook tonight?"

Denise was startled. Sandy never asked to help with any chores. "That's okay. I'm only making spaghetti, but aren't you going to the movies with Gina?"

Sandy shook her head, and her long blonde curls bobbed. "No. Gina's parents

won't let her go because she has too much homework. Maybe we can do something together tonight like you always used to ask when I had plans with my friends."

Those days were long gone, and Denise had gotten used to being a childless parent. "I actually have something to do tonight, honey," she said thinking about her appointment with Pierre.

Sandy shrugged. "Whatever. I guess I'll just play on my iPad."

As she walked away, her brother came through the door. He was carrying his baseball glove and looking glum.

"Ray, What's wrong?" Denise asked.

"My game was canceled. The coach is sick."

"Sorry to hear that. Maybe you can play with one of your buddies in the park."

"Nah. I think I'll just watch some T.V. unless you or dad want to toss me some balls outside, so I can practice my catching."

"I can't," Denise said, "I have something to do on the computer tonight, and I think your father will also be working on his programming."

Just as the younger Raymond left the room, the elder Raymond walked through the front door.

"Guess what, Denise? I'm not working tonight," he announced. "I'd like to have a family meeting."

Denise was puzzled. Years ago, when the kids were younger, they used to have monthly family meetings. That tradition had ended as abruptly as it began.

"What is the meeting about? I don't really have the time tonight."

Raymond hung up his jacket in the hall closet. "It won't take long. Have a seat in my office, and I'll go get the kids."

When the family was gathered in Raymond's office, he handed Denise an envelope. "I'm giving you your birthday present a little early, my dear. I wanted the kids to be present for when you open it because it involves them, too."

What was going on? Denise opened the envelope to find four airline tickets to Paris. "Oh, my God! We're going to Paris!" she said thinking of Pierre and how ironic it was that her boring husband would be the one to fulfill her lifelong dream.

Sandy jumped up and down like she was exercising on her

trampoline. "This is cool! Wait till Gina hears. She'll be so jealous."

Ray seemed happy, too. "Maybe I can meet a pretty French girl there," he joked.

Raymond smiled. "I know how much you've always wanted to see Paris, Denise, so I've been working extra-long hours on my programs to afford a trip there for all of us. It'll be nice for the family to spend quality time together for a change."

Denise felt guilty. How could she accept this wonderful gift knowing that, behind Raymond's back, she'd been having an emotional affair with someone else?

"Is something wrong?" Raymond asked seeing her expression. "The kids are eager to go, and I'm also planning to hire a cat sitter to watch Fred, so why that look? Are you in shock?"

"It's a big surprise," she said. "And a very nice one. I just need time to absorb it all."

"Sure thing," Raymond said. "We'll be leaving next week, and I've even booked us a champagne tour of the Eiffel Tower on your birthday."

Denise felt even guiltier. She tried to show some enthusiasm to mask her feelings. "You've thought of everything, Raymond. Thank you so much."

After the kids left, still talking about their upcoming grand Paris adventure, Raymond asked her to stay a few minutes. "Even though our anniversary isn't for another few months, maybe this can be a second honeymoon for us," he said with a twinkle in his blue eyes. "What do you think? You don't need to answer right away, just think about it, Mon Amour."

Mon amour? When did Raymond learn French?

"Oh, and aren't you going to log into Facebook tonight?"

Did Raymond suspect she had an online boyfriend? Maybe

that was why he'd gone to so much trouble getting her such a perfect birthday gift.

"Well, I expected you to be busy with your work," she said.

"Life is too short for working all the time."

Oh, no! Could Raymond have been diagnosed with an incurable disease?

"Why don't we log on to Facebook together?" he suggested. "I think Pierre has something to confess."

Now she was really panic-stricken. "Pierre? You know Pierre?"

Raymond grinned. "You could say I know him very well, Mon Amour, and I also know a lot about you that I never discovered during all our years of marriage."

"Oh, Raymond, I'm so sorry. I never meant anything by it, but Pierre was sweet and charming. He was just a good friend. I swear."

"Would you have visited him in Paris had he sent you tickets?"

"I don't know. I never really planned to meet him in person. I just liked to talk with him, but Paris is such a beautiful and romantic city. I haven't been away on a vacation since the children were babies."

"Exactly. That's why I thought this would be such a nice gift. And, although I sense your hesitancy about meeting Pierre in the flesh, you already have."

"What? How can that be?" Denise was even more confused.

"You're looking at him," Raymond pointed at himself. "I'm sorry if I misled you, but for the last year I sensed you were getting bored with me, and I couldn't blame you. After a certain number of years of marriage, it's common for the excitement to wear off. I wanted to revive that. I made up Pierre after you told me you joined the Online Artists' group. I found it easier talking to you online and was able to show you the romantic side I often hide. I hope you can forgive me for the masquerade. I never expected it to go on this long. I thought you'd figure it out on your own. I was surprised you never questioned why Pierre never posted a Facebook photo. I guess you thought he was shy."

Denise couldn't believe her husband was her virtual dream man. "I think I can forgive you," she finally said. "But maybe next year I'll join an Italian group, so you can take me to Venice."

He winked, "It would be Giovanni's pleasure, Signora."

Debbie De Louise is an award-winning author and a reference librarian at a public library on Long Island. She is a member of Sisters-in-Crime, International Thriller Writers, the Long Island Authors Group, and the Cat Writers' Association. Her novels include the five books and three stories of the *Cobble Cove* cozy mystery series, a comedy novella, *When Jack Trumps Ace*, a paranormal romance, *Cloudy Rainbow*, and the standalone mysteries; *Reason to Die*, *Sea Scope*, and *Memory Makers*. Her latest book, *Pet Posts: The Cat Chats* is a non-fiction pet book. She lives on Long Island with her husband, daughter, and three cats.

Debbie's stories and poetry also appear in the *Red Penguin Collections, What Lies Beyond* and *'Tis the Season*. Her poems are also featured in the Nassau County *Voices In Verse* 2020 anthology and the 2020 *Bards Annual*.

https://debbiedelouise.com

ABOUT THE AUTHOR

JK Larkin is a Long Island based writer and recent graduate of Marymount Manhattan College. On top of his position as Literary Manager and Editor of *The Red Penguin Collection*, JK works at The Mary Louis Academy as the coach of their Speech & Debate Team, coaching students to perform excerpts of dramatic literature, prose, and poetry for weekly competitions on both the local and national levels. His body of work draws heavily upon themes of existentialism, morality, and the struggle to connect in a deeply divided world. This past year, JK published his first two collections, *not kidding.* and *Side Street*. Follow him at @jksnotkidding on Instagram or @JKLarkinTM on Facebook to keep up to date with his artistic journey.

ALSO FROM THE RED PENGUIN COLLECTION

Realiteen: Reflections On Growing Up

What Lies Beyond: Sci-Fi Stories of the Future

A Trip For The Books

I Can't Find My Flashlight

The Moments

The Beauty Within—Stories of Spirituality, Faith and Love

'Tis The Season—Poems to Lift Your Holiday Spirits

We Made It!—Essays Reflecting On The New Year

Stand Out—The Best of the Red Penguin Collection, Vol. 1

It's The End Of The World As We Know It

Feeding The Flock—Recipes from the Red Penguin Family

www.ingramcontent.com/pod-product-compliance
Lightning Source LLC
Chambersburg PA
CBHW030436120726
47903CB00003B/985